D0375174

The Saver

The Saver

EDEET RAVEL

GROUNDWOOD BOOKS | HOUSE OF ANANSI PRESS
TORONTO   BERKELEY

Groundwood Books / House of Anansi Press
110 Spadina Avenue, Suite 801, Toronto, Ontario M5V 2K4
or c/o Publishers Group West
1700 Fourth Street, Berkeley, CA 94710

We acknowledge for their financial support of our publishing program the
Canada Council for the Arts, the Government of Canada through the Book
Publishing Industry Development Program (BPIDP), and the
Ontario Arts Council.

Library and Archives Canada Cataloguing in Publication
Ravel, Edeet
The saver / Edeet Ravel.
ISBN-13: 978-0-88899-882-8 (bound).–ISBN-13: 978-0-88899-883-5 (pbk.)
ISBN-10: 0-88899-882-1 (bound).–ISBN-10: 0-88899-883-X (pbk.)
I. Title.
PS8585.A8715S29 2008   jC813'.54   C2008-902513-X

Cover photograph: Design Pics © 2008
Design by Michael Solomon
Printed and bound in Canada

For my nephew, Joshua, with love

Monday
November 19

Hi Xanoth,

OK, I know you aren't real. I'm not a psycho or anything.

But I like thinking about you. I like thinking about your violet eyes and how beautiful your planet is. I love how it's so clean and perfect, there isn't even a word for garbage in your language.

I've been thinking about you since the year after I had Mrs. Johnston. I had her in grade four, when I was ten. Then in grade five everything went back to being messed up. I didn't even see Mrs. Johnston in the hall, because she retired right after I had her.

So starting in grade five, to keep myself awake in class and to help me fall asleep at night, I began thinking about you. That means I've been thinking about you for seven years. By now I know a million things about your reality – your glass dome houses, the swan gardens, your job as a pilot flying people from place to place, and how everything is free on your planet. And you can eat whatever you want, because the food is made with special ingredients that aren't fattening but taste exactly the same, only better.

Anyhow, I'm writing to you now because down here on Earth my mom died. I came home from school and Julian, the tenant with the white triangle beard in Apartment 2, opened his door. I thought he was going to go on one of his rants about how we're leaving food lying around and that's why there's cockroaches in the building. Julian has a roach obsession. He has a million bug traps in his apartment, and he puts sticky paper around his bed at night because he's terrified the roaches are going to crawl over his face while he's asleep. So as soon as he hears anyone on the stairs, he pokes his head out and begins shouting that people are leaving food out and not tying up their garbage in bags.

But today, just as I was getting ready to block him out of my mind, he said, "Your mother's in the hospital. She fell on the stairs. I called 911 and an ambulance came to get her."

I felt unbelievably sick. If you asked me how I'd feel if I got home and found out my mother fell on the stairs and had to be taken to the hospital in an ambulance, I would have said I'd be OK. But I felt really sick, like I was going to throw up, only worse.

Meanwhile Julian kept repeating over and over like a parrot, "I called 911, I called 911," like he's waiting for me to notify all the papers so they can put him on the front page, or like calling 911 is going to erase from my reality the ten million times he yelled at me and Mom.

I didn't want him to see how sick I felt. I said, "What

hospital did they take her to?" and he said, "I called 911 and they came and took her to the Montreal General."

I didn't say anything. I just continued up the stairs to our apartment.

I unlocked our door and put down my knapsack, which was empty apart from my wallet and my library book, *Murder Times Nine*. That's what I do at school when I'm not sleeping. I sit in the corner and read mysteries. In Sunnyview, if you're quiet, the teachers are just happy they don't have to relate to you. Sunnyview has the worst kids in the city. There are lots of messed-up people on Earth, Xanoth.

As soon as she heard me come in, Beauty, my cat, came running over. I picked her up and went to the kitchen to grab something before I went to the hospital. But I was too sick to eat, so I packed two bags of vinegar chips, in case I got hungry later. Then I put Beauty down. She didn't understand why I was going out again. She didn't like being left alone, especially because she knew something was wrong, but I didn't have a choice.

I wasn't sure how to get to the Montreal General, so I took the bus to the metro and asked the guy in the booth. He said I had to go to Lionel Groulx, switch to the green line, get off at Guy, and take either the 165 or the 166.

It all went OK until I got off the bus. The driver told me that was the stop for the hospital, but I couldn't see a hospital anywhere. I kept crossing back and forth at this crazy intersection of like six streets. It was freezing cold, and the wind was blowing in my face so I couldn't see anything, and I almost got run over.

Finally I asked this woman who looked like a nurse. She told me the hospital was the building at the top of the hill, and she explained how to get to the entrance. I don't know who thought of putting a hospital in a place no one can get to.

I was a solid block of ice by the time I found the door. I stood at the entrance for a few minutes just to thaw out. I was hungry, even though I still felt sick. I wasn't in the mood for chips, and I had three dollars, so I got a Reese bar from a machine they had there. I wanted two bars, but I didn't want to be left without any money at all. I didn't think to take more from the tin before I left.

No one knew where my mother was. They didn't have any record of a Felicity Henderson, and I started thinking maybe Julian made it all up, or got the wrong hospital. I know on your planet no one gets sick, Xanoth, but here the hospitals are packed to the brim, and people were getting impatient with me because the phones were ringing and everyone was busy.

They sent me to another desk and then to a third desk, and finally this old wrinkly woman at the third desk was nice. I never saw anyone with so many wrinkles, really deep and crossing every which way, but she was friendly and happy. She said, "Don't worry, dear. If she's here we'll find her."

She checked her computer and finally she found

Mom. I could tell right away that she found her on the dead people list. She didn't want to say anything, but I knew from the look on her face.

She told me to wait in Room 203 and someone would be with me soon.

Room 203 was one of those dead empty rooms with a poster of palm trees that's supposed to make you forget there aren't any windows. There weren't even old gross magazines to look at. I had my library book with me, but I knew I wouldn't be able to concentrate on it.

I ate the chips I brought in my knapsack. Then I shut my eyes and thought about you in your glass dome, having lemon meringue pie while your nieces and nephews played on the swings in the back lawn.

Finally a social worker came in – one of those superior types you feel like killing on the spot. Around 25, with big brown sadistic eyes. Her clothes matched her personality. She was wearing a long tight skirt that was kind of worm-beige and made of some horrible polyester, and a blue shirt with buttons that was even worse, and a black suit jacket with a pocket.

She said, "Dr. Gupta is on his way. I'm sorry we have some bad news," but she was really happy, believe me.

I didn't want to give her the pleasure of telling me the bad news, so I said right away, "I guess my mother's dead."

She nodded and pretended she wanted to put her arm around my shoulders to comfort me, but I wouldn't let her. Then Dr. Gupta, this dark-skinned guy with glasses, came in. He had the most boring voice in the world. Even if you wanted to concentrate on what he was saying, you couldn't. He should have been a teacher. So I don't really know what he said, but it had something to do with Mom's heart.

When he left, the social worker gave me a Baggie with Mom's necklace inside. It's a thin gold chain with a small moon pendant. Mom never took it off, even when she showered.

I unzipped the pocket of my knapsack and stuffed the Baggie inside and zipped it up again, which at least gave me something to do. The social worker said, "They did everything they could, but it was a massive heart attack." I could tell she really liked saying "massive."

Then she asked me if there was anyone I could call – a relative or a friend. She wanted to get rid of me so she could move on to her next job of telling someone their whole family was dead in a car crash.

I didn't know what to say. On the one hand, I didn't want to give her the pleasure of knowing there wasn't anyone I could call, and on the other hand, there wasn't anyone. All I have is an uncle out west, but I think he's in prison.

So I just kept saying, "Everyone I know is in Manitoba," and finally she got bored and asked me how old I was, because someone had to identify the body and fill in all the forms. I lied and said 18. Luckily she didn't ask for proof. She only asked if I was ready to see Mom.

I felt like saying, no, I'm not ready, I need to strangle you first. But of course I said yes.

Even if she hadn't needed me to identify Mom, I would have asked to see her. I wanted to make sure she was really dead, and that they didn't make a mistake. If I didn't see her, I'd always wonder about that.

I guess somewhere in the back of my mind I was thinking that maybe it wasn't her, maybe someone else's mother was the one who died. That happens sometimes in mysteries, like in *Simisola*, by Ruth Rendell. The detective calls the parents to identify their daughter, and it turns out it's not her. But that's because the daughter's black, and the police jump to conclusions, because a black girl the same age is missing.

I knew that wasn't going to happen to me. If it wasn't my mom, they wouldn't have the necklace.

The social worker told me she'd be back in a minute, but I couldn't wait in that room from hell again, so I waited out in the corridor.

While I was standing there, leaning against the wall, an Asian family of about a million people showed up. They were all talking at the same time and looking for something. Finally they went into the same room I was in. I guess that's the waiting-to-hear-someone-died room. I felt bad for them at first, but they were smiling and laughing, so maybe they hated the person who died, and now they were going to inherit a lot of money.

A few minutes later the social worker came back and took me to a very creepy place. It was just like in a movie, a dead body on a table. The only difference was that the sheet covering Mom had blue flowers on it, and she had a pillow under her head. Her skin was like pale stone, but apart from that she looked the same, with her beautiful eyes and flat eyebrows and her perfect nose and mouth, and her black hair parted in the middle. I didn't inherit her nose or her mouth, unfortunately. I only inherited her eyes, but on her they looked good. On me they're a waste.

Suddenly I was all dizzy, like I was going to faint, and the social worker said, "Do you want a few minutes alone with your mother?" That was the last thing I wanted. It wasn't her anyhow.

"I just need a bathroom," I said. I was mad at myself because my voice was all crackly.

The social worker took me to a bathroom that smelled of puke. There was a smell of bleach too, but it couldn't get rid of the smell of puke. So I got out of there right away. I decided to focus on you and not think about anything else for now.

The social worker wasn't there when I came out. I waited for her on a chair, and finally she came rushing back, mumbling some lame excuse. She probably went outside to smoke. I noticed a bit of a bulk in her jacket pocket, and she was sucking on a mint, and her cheeks were a bit red. I'm good at clues, maybe from all the mystery books I read.

She asked for the millionth time whether I had any relatives or friends of the family, and I had to tell her for the millionth time that it was only my mother and me in Montreal, so she spelled out all the options. I was barely listening. But one option was donating Mom to McGill University, and that's what I chose. It's free, and that way the hospital looks after everything, even the death certificate.

She said there were a lot of forms to fill in, and I'd need to come back and bring my mother's birth certificate and social insurance card and driver's license. Like someone like us would have a car.

She told me I had to bring my birth certificate too. What if she finds out I'm only 17?

Then she checked her sadistic date book and made an appointment for me for tomorrow at 3:30. She also gave me a flyer, *When a Loved One Dies*, but she said most of it didn't apply to me, because the hospital would take care of everything. Her nails had this worm-beige polish on them, to match her skirt. What a loser.

I thought I was through with her, but she started again with all her fake "What will you do, where will you go?" What she was really thinking about was probably her boyfriend, and how she's going to get into spiked boots with him tonight.

She gave me a number I could reach her at. She kept on and on about how she didn't want me to be alone, so finally I told her I'd stay at my best friend's house, and I gave the address of one of the places where Mom cleans. Cleaned. I got up to go, and she made me promise to call her tonight. In your dreams, Miss Muffet.

I took the bus and metro and bus back home, and I made myself spaghetti and scrambled eggs and a tuna sandwich with mayonnaise. I don't eat cows or pigs. Mrs. Johnston, the teacher I had in grade four, said she never ate mammals because mammals have souls like humans, and all the same emotions as humans, even hope. She said she wouldn't eat a horse or a dog or a cat, so why would she eat cows? She's right about emotions, because look at Beauty.

Then I wanted dessert, so I lifted the cake cover, not really expecting anything, but there was a whole new orange cake there. I guess Mom made it in the morning, before she left for work.

So that's when it hit me, I guess. I sliced the cake and ate it and I was crying my lungs out. I wasn't worried about anyone hearing me, because downstairs they always have the TV on full-blast, and on our floor it's only bikers and skinheads. Beauty didn't know what was going on. She kept jumping on my lap, then going to her bowl to see if there was food in it, then jumping on my lap again.

I turned on the TV to get my mind off things. The show really sucked and the reception was messed up as usual because we don't have cable, but it was that or nothing.

I don't even know what the show was about. My mind kept turning off. Some guy was saying he was innocent, and some beautiful blond woman was helping him, and every few minutes they showed a kid on a tricycle. Each time my mind turned off, I missed a big chunk of the story, and even though you can usually tell what's going on because they repeat the plot about a hundred times, I couldn't figure it out. I gave up and shut the TV.

One thing I know for sure. I'm not going back to Sunnyview. I flunked grade five, so I repeated, and I flunked again, but you can only get held back once. That's the rule. Otherwise they'd have all these old kids in classes with little kids. If you flunk twice, they basically leave you alone. You can go to special dummy classes if you want, but you don't have to. You can sit with everyone else and no one bothers you.

Now that I'm 17 I don't have to go to school at all. I've only been going this year because there wasn't anything else to do. Ricardo, the guy I went out with in grade nine, switched to another school, so I didn't have to see him. As for everyone else, I figured out years ago how to be invisible. You just ignore people who are mean to you and they get bored, because people like to be noticed. And if you don't notice them, they'll move on to someone who does notice.

Besides, I'm strong. I'm stronger than a lot of the guys and I'm pretty good at using my elbows if the need arises. If you use your elbow it's like, oh sorry, did my elbow accidentally poke your eye out? Not that I actually say anything. The main survival strategy is never to say a thing. Silence is the ultimate weapon. A lot of people don't know that.

I decided to have a shower and go to bed. As usual the water pressure was non-existent and the water kept going cold every few seconds. It was the last straw of today. If it wasn't for Beauty, I would have taken a hammer and smashed the faucets, but I didn't want to scare her, so I just cried. Then I put on my sweatpants and a T-shirt and got into bed. Beauty jumped up and sat next to me, the way she always does. I tried reading *Murder Times Nine* but I couldn't concentrate.

So I decided to write and tell you about today. I'm writing in a really nice notebook that Simone, the woman who lived with us until I was seven, sent me five or six Christmases ago. It has pressed flowers on the cover. I didn't have anything to write in it until now, just like I've never had anything to write on a computer. I could have set up an email address in the library, but who would I write to? All I'd get is mail saying YOUR SMALL PENIS WILL SOON BE HISTORY. That's what a lot of companies use email for down here on Earth.

The whole time I've been writing, Beauty's been putting her paw on the paper as if she wants to write too.

Well, that was my day, Xanoth. What I really wanted to tell you is that I was a total bitch to Mom this past year. And my last words to her were, "Leave me alone."

She said, "Wait, Fern, you forgot your pass," because she saw last month's bus pass on the counter and she thought it was this month's. I didn't bother explaining. I just said, "Leave me alone." And now she really did.

Yours forever,
Fern

Tuesday
November 20

Hi Xanoth,

This morning I woke up with my pillow and hair all sticky and gross from crying. I remembered right away about Mom. Beauty was purring next to me, as if she was trying to make me feel better.

I turned on the radio and washed my hair and changed my pillowcase. I had breakfast and then I took out the shoebox where Mom kept all the documents and brought it to the table.

All her things were there – her birth certificate from Manitoba and her social insurance card and some brochures from the government that Dr. Cooper, one of the people she cleaned for, gave her. She never bothered with any of those brochures, but she kept them anyhow. They were all about special deals for First Nations, but Mom was scared of anything to do with forms.

It was horrible seeing her name on everything. It was like she didn't matter anymore, and it didn't matter what her name was. I can't really explain. It was like her name didn't even exist, or like that's all that was left of her, and

Felicity Henderson were just two words that didn't mean anything.

I thought I knew everything in the box, but there was a postcard from Mom's brother that she didn't tell me about. He sent it in July, so it looks like he's not in jail anymore. The postcard is from a place called Brandon in Manitoba, and it has four different photos, probably because each one alone is too boring to be a whole postcard – a fountain and an old building and a church and a park.

On the back it says,

Dear Felicity, How are you and Fern? You are both in my heart and thoughts. I moved here a short while ago and got a job. I'm on the right path now and hope to come down for a visit when I can. Lots of love and hugs, Jack.

Then he gave his address. I'm going to have to write and tell him about Mom.

Jack's the only person in Mom's family. They got adopted together on a farm in Manitoba, mostly so they could help out. Mom was six and Jack was eight. Before that they were on a reserve.

My birth certificate was in the box too. For "father's name" Mom left it blank, even though she knew my father's name. He worked on the farm, but he ran away when he found out she was having me. He was from some place like Norway or the Netherlands. His name was Ted Nielsen. Mom says I look a lot like him. Poor guy.

I put the documents in my knapsack and then I checked the money in the tin. We never had a bank account, because the bank charges you if you're poor, so Mom kept the spending money in a Christmas tin and the rent money in a pair of socks.

You're lucky there's no money on your planet, Xanoth, and no such thing as crime. We got robbed twice, but they didn't find the tin or the socks, because Mom kept them both in the laundry hamper, under a lot of dirty laundry. The trick is to put a white handkerchief with tomato sauce stains right on top. Then if any thieves look inside the hamper, they think it's blood, and they get grossed out and don't bother emptying it. Simone, the woman who lived with us when I was small, taught us that trick. There wasn't much Simone didn't know.

The only thing the thieves took the first time was a watch I got Mom for Christmas. There wasn't anything else worth taking. Even the watch was only $12.96 plus tax. They unplugged the VCR but changed their minds about stealing it, I guess because it's all DVDs now.

The second time we got robbed was when I was in grade six. They took a lot of food, about $160 worth. Beauty couldn't stop meowing the second time. It was like she was saying, "I'm sorry I let someone take all the food." She's so smart! I wasn't worried about her, because she hides when anyone comes to the door.

After those robberies I put a sign on the door, BEWARE OF DOG, but the bikers tore it off. We didn't have any more break-ins though, probably because it got around that there was nothing to take.

Anyhow, there's $55.23 in the tin and there's rent money for December and January in the socks. Mom always made sure we had rent for the two months ahead.

If I don't pay on December 1, it'll be another month at least before I get kicked out, because we've been paying on time for ten years. If I keep the rent money, that comes to $1195.23 total. My bus pass expires in three weeks, but if I'm not going to school I won't need a pass.

After I looked through the forms, I did some hand-wash and listened to the radio and read *Murder Times Nine*. Then I had lunch and left for the hospital. It was drizzly and foggy outside, but not as windy as yesterday, and not as cold. And I knew how to get there this time. The hospital looks a bit like a castle, actually.

You'd like Montreal, Xanoth. It's got really cool parts, like Old Montreal and Île Sainte-Hélène, and there's a big mountain in the middle of the city, with forests and a giant cross on top that lights up at night. You can't actually walk inside the forests because it's a gay pickup place, but you can walk on the paths. The good thing about Montreal is that it doesn't feel big, even though it is.

I must say everyone was nice at the hospital. I didn't see the social worker. So much for all her are-you-OK. I told you it was fake from fakeland.

There were a million forms to fill in, but I'm the opposite of Mom – I like filling in forms. I like answering questions like your name, your sex, permanent address, date of birth, relation to the deceased. It's like an exam where you know all the answers. I remembered to change the year I was born. No one noticed that it wasn't the same as my birth certificate.

A skinny guy was in charge of the forms. He had a sort of stutter, but it was the kind that comes from trying to do too many things at once. He kept apologizing in this funny way. He felt bad for me, and he thanked me about a hundred times for donating Mom's body. I don't know why. She's dead, so what does it matter? I liked him. Why wasn't he the social worker?

When I got home I really wished I had someone to call. I even thought of calling Ricardo, the guy I went out with in grade nine. Luckily I don't know his number anymore, or I would have caved in. And it would have been a stupid, desperate thing to do, because how is it going to help to call a guy who made you feel like a speeding train crashed into you? I'm over Ricardo now, but I still get a bit trembly when I think of him, and hearing his voice would probably bring it all back.

I thought of trying to find my uncle's number in Brandon, if he has one, but what would I say? I don't even know him.

I had spaghetti and two cucumber sandwiches and ice cream, and then I started crying about Mom and about

EDEET RAVEL

how I couldn't send Mrs. Johnston a Christmas card when I was in grade five because she went to live with her sister in Ontario and the school didn't know the address, and how by now maybe she was even dead like Mom.

In a million years I'll never know why Mrs. Johnston liked me, Xanoth. It wasn't fake, because she didn't like everyone. She didn't like this girl Cecily, for example. She didn't like most of the boys either.

It started on the first day of grade four. I was the only one with my hair tied back, because Mom scared me with stories about lice from when she was a kid.

But Mrs. Johnston didn't know my hair was in a ponytail because of lice, and the first thing she said after writing her name on the board was how nice it was that my hair was tied back neatly, and how she hated hair falling all over the place. She meant the white kids.

Then she talked about the Queen. She had the Queen's picture on the wall, and she played us a tape of "God Save the Queen." Then she wrote the words on the blackboard, and when the tape was finished she made us all stand up and sing it.

I know that sounds like she was from a bygone era. Maybe she was in some ways, but no one minded and no one laughed. She wasn't the sort of person you laughed at. She had perfect quiet in her classroom. No one shouted out, not even the criminal types who if she was in an alley would grab her purse in two seconds flat. In class she was the ruler. It's just something she had.

Anyhow, I sang really loudly. OK, I was being a suck-up, but I was only a little kid, and it was the first time a teacher said something nice to me. Mrs. Johnston noticed right away and smiled at me.

In case you're wondering what she looked like, she had very neat white hair in waves, rosy cheeks and glasses with light blue frames. She always wore a navy skirt with a white blouse and matching jacket, but with a different scarf and a different pin every day. She said we needed something bright to look at. Her pins were made of rubies and emeralds and diamonds, and they were in the shape of butterflies or fish or just pretty designs, like an oval with emerald teardrops falling from it. No one knew if they were real. I mean, we knew she wasn't rich, but maybe her great-great-grandmother was rich, and the jewels were passed down through the generations.

I even lost weight that year, because one time after class she told me that if I cut down on desserts and soft drinks, she'd give me 5 extra bonus points each month. Every time someone did good work they got a bonus point, and as soon as you had 15 bonus points, you got a prize from the prize bag, like a book of poetry for kids or a joke book or a game, for example those little squares you move around to get them in order. Mrs. Johnston put one hand over her eyes and with the other hand she dug into the prize bag to make it fair, but I think she was feeling for the prize that would fit the kid who was getting it.

I didn't care about the points or the prizes, but I didn't

want her to stop liking me, so I lost around 30 pounds that year. I hate soft drinks anyhow, so that part was easy, and I only let myself have two slices of cake after supper. Two slices and that was it. Every time I stopped at two, I felt I was doing it for Mrs. Johnston, and it was as if she was watching me. All evening I wanted to go to the kitchen and take another slice, but I didn't.

I earned six prizes in all: *The Hound of the Baskervilles*, Rubik's Tangle which is little pictures of ropes that you have to connect, a book about famous women and what they did, eight nature postcards that folded like an accordion, Brain Quest Weird Stuff (Strange, Gross and Unbelievable But True Facts), and a collection of crossword puzzles about cats. I think Mrs. Johnston probably found the prizes in garage sales, but they were in perfect condition.

The class was for dummies, but Mrs. Johnston said that if we didn't understand something it was her fault, not ours, because she wasn't doing a good job explaining it. Like when she was trying to explain to us that four quarters make a dollar and two nickels make a dime – a lot of kids were having trouble with that (as I said, the dummy class), so finally she turned it into a game. She made some kids into pennies and some kids were nickels and some were dimes and quarters, and that was how those kids finally learned it. I was the only dollar.

Every day before the bell she read us another chapter from *Tom Sawyer*. We didn't really know what was going on, but we still liked it. She hated gum chewing. She spent a lot of time on how to use commas. She really drummed it into us about commas. Commas and apostrophes. And capital letters and indent. To indent you put two fingers on the page. She liked cucumber sandwiches. That's what she ate for lunch every day. She was skinny. She made us sign a pledge that we would never smoke, and she gave us all the reasons why smoking was bad. She said it was like drinking from a lake that had gasoline and tar and sewage flowing into it. And if you thought that was disgusting then it didn't make sense to smoke, because you were doing the exact same thing as drinking from that lake. She always used to say "You're right, I'm wrong" when she made a mistake. She had a principle about that.

I wish real life had points. Points for every time you did the laundry and went shopping and didn't throttle someone. Then when you had 100 points, the President of the World would send you a computer, or a car.

I'm going to sleep now, even though it's early. Beauty is sleeping right next to me, with her head on the pillow like a human.

Yours forever,
Fern

EDEET RAVEL

Wednesday
November 21

Hi Xanoth,

I had a lot of really bad dreams last night. They started off with the story in *Murder Times Nine*, which is about nine people who get murdered one by one, and the detective is trying to find the connection between them. But then everything changed in the dream and it got very weird and scary.

I finally woke up. I made breakfast and then I called Sunnyview and told them I wasn't coming back. The secretary took the message.

I also wrote to my uncle. I just said,

Hi Jack. I'm sorry to have to tell you that Mom died. Felicity, I mean. I don't know if you're still at this address. I also don't know how long I'll be staying here, so if you write back send your letter to 301 Prince Albert in Westmount. I don't know the postal code but you can look it up. It's one of the places where Mom cleaned. Your niece, Fern.

I put it in an envelope from the junk mail downstairs.

I crossed out VISA and wrote Jack's address instead. All I needed was a stamp.

I don't even know what Jack looks like. Mom has two photos of him, but in one he's a kid and the other is from too far to see much.

After that I had to do something. I knew if I sat around the house all day, I'd go crazy. So I decided to go to work instead of Mom. Apart from giving me something to do, I'd get paid.

Also it's Wednesday, and every second Wednesday she cleaned for the Coopers, which is where I told Jack to write. Mom didn't go last week, which meant they were expecting her today. I figured if I went there I'd be able to tell them in person that I gave Jack their address, and I could ask them for a stamp.

The Coopers live in a big old house in Westmount. They're very quiet. They had a daughter who died. Her picture is over the fireplace. They aren't too interested in anything and there's never much to clean at their place. It wasn't the first time I was going instead of Mom. I took her place whenever she was sick or had a migraine.

They're nice old people, tall and skinny. People who are that nice make you feel bad. Dr. Cooper worked in Africa, but he's retired now.

They've always helped us out. They paid our phone bill because you can't pay without a bank account. Mom gave them the money and they looked after it. They also offered to apply for benefits for her, but she said no. She didn't want anything to do with the government.

There was a bit of snow this morning, but it turned into rain and fog before I got to the Coopers. I like fog.

I got there at around 11. They told me to help myself to whatever I wanted for lunch. I told them I gave Jack their address because we might be moving, and I asked if they had a stamp. They took the letter and promised to mail it. They asked how Mom was. I said she was taking a day off.

They always go out on cleaning day to visit some old friends. After they left, I made myself three kinds of sandwiches – cold chicken and lettuce, peanut butter and margarine, peanut butter and jam. The bread was the kind you slice yourself.

Then I found a bag of old sprouting potatoes. They were OK once I peeled them. I boiled a few and mashed them with margarine. Then I had spiral cinnamon cookies that were pretty stale, and chocolate milk. I really like chocolate milk. I'd drink it five times a day if I could afford it.

After I ate I cleaned the house cleaner than it's ever been in its entire life. I moved these old big sofas and cleaned behind and under them and I got out a stepladder and cleaned the light fixtures. They were really dusty. Then I did all the windows and windowsills, though I couldn't do the outside. Wonder Woman, that's me.

I stayed a lot longer than I was supposed to, and I was

still working away for two hours after they got back. They were surprised, I think. They gave me a big tip, $40 on top of the $60, and they said they hope Mom gets well soon.

Dr. Cooper said, "She must be extremely proud of you." I let him have his illusion.

I'm wiped out from lifting sofas and moving beds. I hope I won't have those dreams tonight. I'll think about your planet, Xanoth, and the vegetable gardens and the pink and blue skies and cute sheep. Did you have fun at the outdoor dance with the crystal lights on the trees and the rainbow stars against the dark sky? Did your sister Lulu set the date for her wedding? I wonder where she and Om will go on their honeymoon, and how many children they'll have. I love how it doesn't hurt to give birth on your planet. The babies just slip out, and instead of crying when they come out, they laugh.

Yours forever,
Fern

Thursday
November 22

Hi Xanoth,

I should explain that I can't tell anyone about Mom because of the rent. Julian, the guy who called 911, asked how she was doing. I said we switched hospitals, just in case he gets it into his mind to check up on me. He asked which hospital, but I pretended not to hear. I'm good at going deaf on people.

The thing is, if they find out Mom's dead they'll kick me out of here right away. They've been dying to kick us out because they want to double or triple the rent.

But they always wait before they take action on a late tenant, because taking action costs money, and then if you pay the rent they lose that money. Since we've always been on time, they won't want to take action for nothing. So I can stay at least until the end of December without paying the December rent. That gives me time to plan what I'll do next.

It was really windy and cold today, with rain turning into ice. But I went to clean a house anyhow, just to get my mind off things while I figure out what to do. I had bad dreams again, by the way. So I went to the Thursday-Saturday house.

Insane people live there. It's amazing how people can be part of society and everything, and be completely insane inside their house. The husband, Mr. Dixler, teaches at university, and his wife teaches aerobics at the Y, so you'd think they'd be normal, but they're not. They have four kids. All the kids are crazy too, probably because of their parents.

I love how no one is gross on your planet, Xanoth, and you don't even have a word for disgusting because you don't know what it is. Here on Earth it's very different.

For one thing, no one in that house flushes the toilet. I don't understand that part. I don't get how they don't mind going to the toilet and being forced to see other people's dumps. They have four bathrooms and it's the same in all of them.

But that's just a small detail. The whole house is a lunatic asylum, dark, filthy, with a million old appliances and tools and probably torture instruments lying all over the place. Just piles of strange things on the floor, which you have to step over as you walk. There's a TV screen the size of a whole wall in the living room and flat screen TVs in every room. They have locks on the outside of all the kids' doors, so the kids can get locked in when they're bad, and their rooms are full of skulls and pet snakes and scorpions in jars and posters from every horror movie ever made, including some they drew themselves.

On top of all that, the place is teeming with cock-roaches, and it's a new house. It's new and enormous and probably cost three million dollars, but it's even more wrecked than our building. The whole house smells because of the weird snakes and rotting food, and because of their chihuahua, who sometimes goes in the corner and no one bothers cleaning it up. When no one's home the chihuahua goes to a daycare for dogs, so at least he has a break from the family.

The only time I cleaned this house before was on Saturday, when most of them were home. I won't even try to describe what that was like, with the chihuahua going completely crazy, and every single TV on a different station, plus they put on music, plus they shouted nonstop.

There's three boys and a girl. One of the boys and the girl are twins, I think, around ten, and the other two boys are older. They were all fighting with each other and with their parents. None of their arguments made sense. It's like they were all talking about different things, but they acted as if they were on the same topic.

I spent the whole day hiding in the laundry room. Even the laundry room had this big poster of a giant stuffing the arm of a small man inside his mouth. He's already bitten off the head and there's blood everywhere. The poster was from an exhibition of an artist called Goya. The one art poster they have, and it has to be of a cannibal eating a human head. I had to concentrate the whole day on not looking at it.

I did a million loads of laundry, filling the machine, then the dryer, then folding everything. In between, I cleaned the laundry room. That kept me busy until it was time to go. They didn't care what I did. I think they all have ADD.

After that Saturday, I didn't want to go back, so when Mom was sick I just called and said she wasn't coming. I wouldn't have gone today either if it was a Saturday, but on Thursdays the kids are at school and the parents are at work and the dog's at daycare.

It's hard to get to their house. They live in TMR, which is a rich people's area, and the bus doesn't run on most of the streets, probably because everyone in TMR has cars. It's nine blocks from the bus stop to the Dixlers. By the time I got there, I could barely move my fingers to unlock the door. They keep the key under a fake rock next to a fake plant. Obviously they could never keep a real plant alive.

There isn't much you can do in a place like that, and there's no point anyhow, because they wouldn't notice. All you can do is fill the sink with soap and water and collect the dishes and ashtrays from all over the house and let them soak in batches and then wash them.

When the dish rack was full, I took a towel out of the closet to put more dishes on. The towel was covered with dog hair and gross stains, like dried mud only yellow, and it smelled like barf from hell. I used it anyhow. It's not my problem if that's how they want to live. I'm not the one who has to eat off those dishes. I didn't even touch them. I brought Mom's rubber gloves with me and believe me I kept them on.

After the dishes were done, I went around the house and collected apple cores and food containers and other garbage in a big garbage bag. I couldn't even look at the things I was throwing out. I knew there was a lot more under the beds, but probably even they're scared to look there. As far as cleaning, it's impossible. You'd have to get rid of all the junk first.

For lunch I ate a bag of cookies I found. It was safe, because it was still sealed from the store, so the cockroaches couldn't get inside. They have cases of bottled water and the bottles are also sealed, so that was safe too.

Then I opened some cans of corn and peas and baked beans and I ate them straight from the can after scrubbing a spoon with an SOS pad. Everything in the fridge was past the due date. Even the ice cream in the freezer tasted like it had gone bad. I took one bite and had to spit it out in the sink. It tasted like slimy dust.

They left me a note on the counter asking me to do laundry. It was strange, because the wrong words were underlined. It said COULD YOU PLEASE <u>DO</u> THE LAUNDRY IF <u>YOU</u> HAVE TIME? THANKS!

What weirdos. Even their notes are weird.

So anyhow, after doing all the dishes and collecting the garbage I went to the laundry room, but when I picked up a bunch of laundry to put it in the machine, all these horrible slimy bugs began slithering out, and suddenly I thought why for the love of Jesus should I do this? It's completely insane to ask someone to clean a house like this, unless you pay them about a hundred times the regular price.

So I took the $60 on the table and I left a note saying SORRY, MY MOTHER CAN'T COME ANYMORE. I should have underlined *my*. Or *any*. Good luck to them finding some other sucker.

When I got home I took a really long shower and shampooed my hair and then I soaked my jeans and shirt in the tub with detergent. I was glad I didn't smash the faucets with a hammer. The shower was working a bit better this time. At least the water didn't keep going cold on me.

Beauty wanted to dip her paw in the water where my clothes were soaking, but I took her out of the bathroom because I didn't want her to get contaminated. Whenever I'm having a bath, or anything's soaking in the tub, she gets on the ledge and dips her paw in the soapy water and licks the water off her paw. That's also how she drinks from her bowl. She dips her paw in the water and licks it. She can do it very fast when she's thirsty.

What she most likes is to lick water right off my legs or feet. It's so cute. So like if I'm in the bath, she hops on the ledge and I take my foot out for her to lick off all the water with her rough tickly tongue, and then I dip it in again and put it out for her again. I love when she does that. She can do it for a whole hour.

After my shower, I put on a clean shirt and sweatpants. I have about 30 shirts, all of which I bought in the men's section at Value Village. They have thousands of shirts coming in all the time, and you can find really nice ones if you go regularly. I like denim, corduroy, flannel or plain cotton if it isn't too thin. I like plaid if they're purple and olive or blue and gray. The important thing is that they're 100% cotton. I have six pairs of jeans for depending on my weight, also from VV, but they were harder to find. Three are duplicates, because jeans take forever to dry. While one pair is drying, I can wear the duplicate.

I don't know what I'm going to do, Xanoth. I have to come up with something, but I can't think right now. I have to empty my brain of that house first. I'll see if anything's on TV.

Yours forever,
Fern

Friday
November 23

Hi Xanoth,

Today was an incredibly messed-up day.

I did the Friday place. It's three doors down from the Dixler house. That's how Mom got the job. The Dixlers recommended her, or else this family recommended her to the Dixlers. I forget which one came first.

This family is the opposite of the Dixlers. Their house is like a palace. I rang the bell, because sometimes the mom is home and sometimes she isn't. No one answered, so I let myself in. They have a special lock that you can only open with a code. The code is 0000. Spooky.

The house is clean but messy. They have three teenage girls, and those kids have everything. They have half a shopping mall in their rooms, except for the youngest. Her room is mostly empty, but it's still beautiful, with Japanese paintings on the wall and a four-poster bed and her collection of carved boxes and tiny glass animals. The other two girls probably don't even know what they have. There are laptops all over the house, and all sorts of other computer-type machines that look like they're from the

future. The father makes them or invents them or something.

The parents have money to burn. There's even a bowl
of loonies and toonies on the hall table, in case they run
out of change.

The furniture is the kind you see in ads for fancy
hotels, all shiny and curvy, with gold along the edges. You
have to take your shoes off before you go in.

The oldest sister, Debbie, left a million instructions
on the kitchen table about cleaning the furniture and all
the different floors and carpets. She put the bottles and
things on the table, and she explained what to use on
what, in very neat handwriting, with words underlined,
as if Mom was stupid and hadn't been cleaning their
house for years.

That note got me so mad I wanted to write something
sarcastic on the paper and just walk out. Like, SORRY,
BUT THESE INSTRUCTIONS WERE TOO COMPLICATED
FOR ME. GOTTA GET BACK TO MY FINGER-PAINTING.

But I was already there and I need the money, so I
decided to ignore the note. At least she underlined the
right words.

I started in the kitchen. When the mom's home I have
to watch what I eat, but when she's out, like today, I can
dive right in. They have a whole room off the kitchen
where they store food, and they have like an entire super-
market there, including a freezer the size of a fridge. A lot
of the stuff is organic. That means no pesticides, which I

know you don't have on your planet, Xanoth, but here they put pesticides on everything, unless you pay double and then you can buy without.

I heated up a pesto pizza and part of a BBQ chicken, and then I sampled some salads from the fridge. They had six different salads, the kind you get at bakeries or delis. For dessert I had some tiny pastries and a big bar of chocolate with almonds and a few slices of a mixed berry pie. They didn't have chocolate milk, but they had chocolate powder from Switzerland, which I had with milk.

Finally I got to work. I started off with the kitchen, mostly doing dishes and wiping the counter. Everything wipes clean in that house. Then I did the bathrooms. There's always a lot of dirt behind toilets, for some reason. Then I emptied the garbage pails in all the rooms.

I was bringing back the pail to one of the bedrooms when suddenly I couldn't do a thing. I couldn't move. I was going to make the bed, but I sat down instead, on the soft aqua duvet, and I looked around.

The bedroom was the middle girl's. She's really pretty, with dark hair and a big happy smile, and she has all these photos over the bed of her and all her friends hugging and laughing. A lot of the photos are from some kind of horse place, probably a horse camp. She looks around 15 or maybe 16. On top of having parents and a huge house and everything money can buy, she has a million friends.

Her name's Linden. We actually met once. It was in

June, right before school ended, and she came home just as I was leaving. She didn't act like a rich person or a snob or anything. Maybe she felt sorry for me, or maybe she's one of those freak nice kids.

She said, "Hi, are you Felicity's daughter?" and I mumbled, yeah, thinking she would continue past me, but she stood there and went on talking. She said, "Is your mom OK?" and I said, "Just a migraine," and she said, "Hold on, hold on."

She ran upstairs and came back with pills. She said, "These are great for migraines. They really work. They're prescription but anyone can take them."

I looked up at her and I saw how pretty she was, shorter than me but skinny, with this friendly smile and big greenish eyes and black eyebrows. Her mom's from New York and she's famous. She writes all these books, like *Fifty Ways to Leave Your Lover*, *Fifty Ways to Stay in Shape*, *Fifty Ways to Lose Weight*, even though everyone knows there's only one way to lose weight, which is eat less. She's very hyper and she travels a lot. She doesn't have the same last name as her husband. He's Fernández and she's Catchlove. Maybe it's a pen name.

I took the pills and said thanks. She was watching me put on my shoes, so I made some joke about my size 10 feet. She laughed and said, "You remind me of our canoeing instructor at this camp I went to. Annie. Everyone liked her."

I couldn't think what to say. I still couldn't tell if she

was nice or just feeling sorry for me, or both. She said, "I hope Felicity feels better," and I said thanks and started to go, but she asked, "What school do you go to?" I said I went to Sunnyview and she said, "I go to Royal Vale but I hate it. I might switch to Sunnyview."

I looked at her like she was crazy, because no one rich goes to Sunnyview. It's totally ghetto. I said, "If you don't mind being mugged on the back stairs," and she laughed again.

Then I said bye and got out of there before she changed her mind about being nice. You never know when a kid might switch from nice to mean, so I figured end on a high note or whatever.

Those pills really worked, by the way. Mom took them until they ran out. I told her to ask for more, but she didn't. She never asked for anything.

Anyhow, I sat there on Linden's bed and suddenly I just couldn't go on cleaning. I stared at this ceramic sign on her door. It has her name in fancy old-type print, and on top of her name there's a close-up of a beautiful woman with a white face and dark hair and curvy red lips and huge blue eyes. She's holding three tiny white flowers in her long fingers and she has faded gold flowers in her hair.

I can't even describe how jealous I was, looking at that sign, and then at everything in the room, like perfume bottles and scrapbooks and handmade stationery and a million amazing beads in little boxes and a million pens and markers and scarves and velvet purses and a white board that you write things on. On the board it said FIGHT THE GOOD FIGHT, WHEREUNTO THOU ART ALSO CALLED. Kind of random, but who knows. Her closet is walk-in and it's crammed with clothes and shoes and games and a lot of other junk.

I tried to imagine what it was like to have a normal life with a big van and parents and sisters. To have that reality.

Suddenly I wanted to steal something. I couldn't take something they might notice, like a ring. I'd be too scared. Rich people have power. They'd call the police and the police would find out that Mom was dead and I'd have to go to a home for delinquents. But I could take something small, like a bar of rosemary and mint soap.

Mrs. Johnston said everyone has a perfect soul to start with, and your soul protects you and guides you in life. But if you steal, it's like someone took a bite out of your soul, and the hole stays forever and can never be fixed. No matter how many good things you do after that, you'll always walk around with a hole, even when you're sixty. And the more holes you have, the more you'll make bad decisions and do stupid things.

So in the end I decided I wouldn't steal, but I realized I couldn't ever come back to that house. I was too jealous.

I made all the beds and tidied as fast as I could but I didn't dust or vacuum. I hate vacuuming, and the carpets looked fine to me.

I took the $60 and left a note saying the same thing I told the dirty people – that my mother couldn't come anymore. I said she was sick.

Then I decided to take a bag of food and a box of chocolate truffles, because Debbie's note said HELP YOURSELF TO LUNCH, so all I was doing was making my lunch bigger. I also took two toonies from the bowl for bus fare, because they always paid for Mom's bus. I still have my pass, but they don't know that.

I was too tired when I got home to think about anything. I had a nap for around three hours, with Beauty right against my back, purring away like crazy.

It was freezing today, for a change. It also snowed, and this time the snow didn't melt when it hit the ground. Winter has officially started.

Tomorrow I'll take some videos out of the library and spend the day vegging out on the sofa.

If I lived on your planet, Xanoth, we'd have breakfast every morning on the lawn, surrounded by tulips and purple butterflies. We'd have real orange juice and fresh rolls right from the oven with butter melting all over them.

Yours forever,
Fern

Saturday
November 24

Hi Xanoth,

All night the bikers next door were having a party, and apart from the horrible music, the doors kept banging with druggies going in and out. I couldn't sleep, so I read until like five in the morning, when they all collapsed, probably in a drug coma, and it got quiet. I slept most of the day.

I got up because Beauty was hungry. She began reaching up to my night table and playing with my pen so it would fall to the floor and make a noise, but like it wasn't her fault. She's so adorable.

After I filled her plate I made tea. I sat down on the sofa with the tea and chocolate cookies from Linden's house. It was too late to get videos. During the week the library's open late, but on Saturdays it closes at 5:00. I wasn't really in the mood for going out anyhow. It's still snowing, and they said on the radio it's minus ten with the wind chill.

So I just sat there staring into space and stroking Beauty and trying to figure out what to do with my life.

I used to want to look after horses or be a detective. I think I'd be good at solving crimes. I used to imagine all the ways I'd trick people into telling the truth. But you have to go to college to be a detective. As for looking after horses, I don't even think a job like that exists.

If I had looks, I'd try to marry someone rich, or if I was brainy I could be a lawyer or something like that, but those two are totally out, unfortunately.

I started thinking about something Mrs. Johnston said. She told us one time that a million was not as much as people thought. She said it didn't take long to earn $1000 in Canada, and if you did that one hundred times, you were already at $100,000. Then if you do that only ten times, you have a million. She said if you never spent a penny, you could make a million in 15 years, because if you put money in the bank, you get interest, and the money grows. The more money you put in, the higher the interest gets. The problem is that people have to spend what they earn.

I started thinking, even if I didn't get looks or brains, I'm pretty strong. People my size aren't always strong. Usually if you weigh as much as I do, it's mostly flab. But I've always had really strong muscles. I can lift things even guys can't lift, unless they're in sports or doing weights. I think I got that from my father, Ted Nielson. Mom wasn't that strong. She was small and her back was always hurting her.

But Ted was helping out on the farm when she met

him, and Mom said he could carry bales of hay and unload sacks of feed like they were feather pillows. He was tall too, and good with horses. Good at calming them down and good at riding. That's probably where I got my interest in horses. Simone, the woman who once lived with us, used to take me to a farm that had wagon rides and animals for kids to pet. You could hardly drag me away from the ponies.

Anyhow, I'm thinking maybe if I work a lot and don't spend any money, in 15 years I can be a millionaire.

If I had tons of money, I'd buy a house like Linden's, but out in the country instead of in the city, and I'd keep three horses. I'd look after them and ride every day. And I'd have a huge garden full of tulips and pansies and daffodils. I'd buy anything I wanted and I'd have a huge tiled bathroom with a sunken bathtub and I'd soak in it forever. Beauty wouldn't have to balance on the edge. She'd sit right next to me and put her paw in the water whenever she felt like it. And when it got cold I'd go to Egypt and Greece and other exotic lands.

If I was a millionaire I wouldn't be stuck in a dead-end life like my mother, cleaning up other people's dirt just to have enough to eat and pay the rent. And then if you get sick and can't work, you could end up sleeping on cardboard.

All I have to figure out is how not to spend anything.

Some jobs are live-in, like looking after kids, but they don't pay much and you can't take another job, and besides I'd kill myself if I had to be someone's slave. I could probably find a shelter for homeless kids, but there'd be rules and other kids and not much food, and it would only be until the summer, when I turn 18.

A much better idea is to get a job as a janitor.

If I was a janitor I wouldn't have to pay rent. Our building shares a janitor with the big building next door. The janitor, Leonard, lives there for free. He doesn't do much, as far as I can see. He once hired me to help paint a place that had to be ready in a rush. He's a sort of old guy from all the way north, near Hudson Bay. For him minus twenty is warm. He never shuts his blinds and you can always see him cooking or watching TV because his window is the same level as the street. Sometimes his son comes to visit when he's between jobs. A good-looking guy with blond hair. His father calls him a bum.

If I had free rent, all I'd have to do is find a second job that has free food. Fast food restaurants hire just about anyone, but they really watch what you eat there. You're allowed one tiny meal, and that's it. If I looked good, I could work for a wedding caterer and take home the wedding food. They had a show once on TV about how much gets thrown out after weddings and banquets – enough for one person to live on for a few months.

But no one's going to hire me for that. I'd put the guests right off their food. Besides, the point of the show was that they were trying to organize a way to pick up the leftovers for poor people, and maybe by now they organized it.

EDEET RAVEL

It would have to be a restaurant job. I could wash dishes in the kitchen, and then maybe I could get all the food they were throwing out because it has to be fresh the next day.

What do you think, Xanoth? I might as well try. Nothing else to do.

I finished *Murder Times Nine*. I didn't figure it out. This famous math professor is the murderer. He made a mistake in front of a group of nine people, and he had to kill everyone who was there because of how embarrassed he was, even though the irony was that it wasn't a mistake in the end. The clue is right there in the title – Times Nine, like in math.

It was Mrs. Johnston who got me started on murder mysteries. She liked telling us about Sherlock Holmes, and sometimes she got dressed up, like with a cane or an old coat, and she'd bring objects in a shopping bag and empty it on her desk. We had to guess things about her from the clues, and at the bottom of the page we wrote, "Elementary, my dear Watson." When I got my first 15 points, she gave me *Hound of the Baskervilles*. I was hooked after that.

Yours forever,
Fern

Sunday
November 25

Hi Xanoth,

It's the middle of the night and I can't sleep. I had the worst dream. Mom came from the hospital in pieces because I donated her to McGill, and a huge monster was trying to get inside the apartment to eat the pieces, like in the dirty people's poster, and I was trying to push the door hard against it, and at the same time I was trying to find the Accident card from the Mille Bornes pack, which in the dream could keep the monster out.

Mille Bornes is a card game I used to play with Mom. Simone taught us Mille Bornes, and she left us the pack when she moved to Kitchener. She also left us Sorry! and Monopoly. For a long time whenever I saw that Sorry! box on the shelf I thought Simone was saying Sorry! for leaving.

Mom and I used to play Mille Bornes all the time. It's such a lame game, but we really liked it. You have to score 5000 miles with cards that have 25, 50, 75, 100 or 200 miles. But the other person can block you with a Flat Tire, a Stop, a Speed Limit, an Out of Gas or an

Accident. Then you can only get unblocked by a Spare Tire, a Go, an End of Limit, Gasoline or Repairs. You can also protect yourself by certain cards like Extra Tank, Puncture Proof, Right of Way and Driving Ace. It can take a really long time to score the 5000 miles, which is what made it fun.

The only time I saw Mom smile was when we played a game, though even then she smiled at the wrong things. I mean if I smiled because I got a good card, she'd be happy. It made me laugh, the way she didn't want to give me the obstacle cards. I'd say, "Mom, you have to try! It isn't a game if you don't try!" It was the same thing in Monopoly. Like if she owned Champs Élysée I had to tell her to buy de la Paix if she landed on it, and I had to force her to collect rent. Poor Mom. I miss her so much, Xanoth.

I think Beauty knew I had a bad dream because when I woke up she came right up to my chest and sat on me, purring and rubbing her face against my chin.

I didn't want to go back to sleep, so I put on the light and I'm writing to you instead.

I've been thinking some more about saving money, Xanoth. Canada is a very good country. Our planet sucks, and we're probably all going to die soon, when some terrorist drops a nuclear bomb on us or releases deadly bacteria everywhere. But in the meantime there are better and worse places, and Canada is a very good place with lots of things that you can get for free, like library books and clothes and condoms. Not that I need condoms or ever will. I'm just giving an example.

Even the dentist is free for little kids, and then if you don't mind a student plus waiting two years, you can get one free at the hospital. Dr. Cooper told us about that. I've never had a cavity, by the way. At least I got one lucky thing in my life.

Anyhow, clothes you can get at vestiaires, and you can also get coupons from the Salvation Army if you're on their list. Value Village can be expensive, depending on their mood, but if you go on their 50% off day you can find bargains. And there's the dollar store for things like detergent.

Food gets thrown out like crazy in Canada, not only at weddings. You just have to find a way to get to it.

Yours forever,
Fern

Monday
November 26

Hi Xanoth,

Today I went to the library to see if there were ads for jan-
itors in the paper.

I'm lucky there's a library nearby. They have videos
and murder mysteries, and you can take out twenty
books if you want. Luckily they haven't thrown out their
video collection. They probably will one of these days.
Everything's DVD now.

I also like books for little kids. I was wandering
around the library one time and I noticed this book on
the table, *Monster Mama*. With a title like that you want
to know what it's about, so I sat down on the carpet next
to the tiny round table and looked at it.

After that I got kind of addicted to books for little
kids. I liked how in every book the pictures were totally
different. Some of the stories were really cute too. Dogs
looking after babies and the shrink who tells the elephant
parents they're bad parents and one fish two fish and
Mulberry Street and may I be a button on your dress and
the dog who hates the sweater and the boy who feeds the

fish too much and the guy who has to do all these feats to get the princess. It's all coming back, now that I'm telling you about it.

There was one I read not knowing it was going to be all sad, and then suddenly on the last page it's like the saddest thing you've ever read. It was about a girl whose mother sends her to the forest for three days because an army is coming, but when the girl comes back, her mother is already an old woman. I started crying right there in the library. The librarian noticed and she said she also cries when she reads it. I said it was too sad for little kids, but she said little kids don't find it sad, only older people.

To get back to today, I didn't have a lot of luck at the library. They get the *Gazette* there, though you have to wait until the old men are finished with it. But I didn't have to wait too long, because no one wanted the classifieds. Those guys are too old to want anything.

I checked all the jobs for janitor, which they had under SUPERINTENDENT. I got really depressed because they all said EXPERIENCED and they want you to have your own tools and be handy. A lot of them asked for a couple. And they wanted references.

I wrote down some numbers, and when I got home I called the Coopers to ask if they could give me a reference.

Mrs. Cooper answered. I said I was applying for a cleaning job and needed a reference. She said, "Aren't you still in school, dear?"

I said, "I need to help Mom out." She said they'll be

happy to recommend me. She said she'd write a letter "to whom it may concern," and I could also give people her phone number. She was very nice.

I didn't tell her it was for a janitor job, because then I'd have to tell her the truth. And then maybe she'd invite me to live with them, but I'd go crazy with all that sadness and niceness, and I'd feel bad eating their food, seeing how much I eat and how little they eat. Plus I don't think they could afford to have me, even if they live in Westmount. They drive a really old car, and they sleep on an old saggy mattress, and the carpets in their house are all worn. Probably you don't make a lot of money working in Africa.

So at least I have a reference now. It makes an even better impression that it's from a doctor.

But all the places I called, they just took my name, and I could tell they weren't going to call back.

Maybe this whole janitor idea is crazy. Maybe it's always guys or couples like the ads say. And I don't really know how to fix anything, though I could probably figure it out if I had to, or ask somebody, or look it up in the library if I got desperate.

I can't give up yet. Maybe I'll get lucky.

Yours forever,
Fern

Tuesday
November 27

Hi Xanoth,

I was running low on food and cat litter, so I went shopping today. We used to pay for delivery, but you can't not give a tip, and with the tip and tax it's at least $6.

So I decided to make a few trips and stock up while I still have my bus pass. I had nothing else to do.

You're lucky, Xanoth, that food is free on your planet. Everything's expensive down here. When I went shopping with Mom we never bought the really expensive things, like cashews or butter, but we bought some medium things, like ice cream and chips.

But today I realized I can't even buy the medium things. I have to stick to the really cheap food. Luckily I'm the sort of person who can eat the same thing every day. I don't need variety like some people.

My first trip was just cat litter. That stuff is beyond heavy.

The second trip was mostly potatoes, which were on sale for $1.98 for a big bag, and cans of tomato sauce, and Whiskas. Beauty really likes the seafood Whiskas, and it isn't all that more expensive than the No Name, only around $1.50 more for the big size. I don't trust the No Name for cat food.

The third trip was more potatoes and more sauce and bread and bananas and rolled oats in a bag and bread-crumbs and tuna, which luckily was on sale and which I have a good recipe for. Tuna-potato burgers. Simone taught us that recipe.

For my next trip I got cauliflowers, which were also on sale, and milk and carrots and two big jars of peanut but-ter for $5.45 each, and three big bags of flour for $1.88 each, and sugar. Finally on my last trip I got a ton of pasta. The No Name was $4.10 for a big bag, which is cheaper than at the dollar store. I was trying to decide if I could afford the chicken. I stood there for about half an hour staring down at the chicken, picking it up, putting it down, sticking it in my cart, taking it out again. In the end I didn't buy it. It's almost $8 for a small chicken and it only lasts one day. I'll wait for a special.

I also didn't buy beans and chickpeas and lentils because there's a place on Sherbrooke that sells things like that in bulk. I'll go there tomorrow. Beans and chickpeas take forever to cook, but you can get a lot of meals out of a small amount.

I'm also running low on toilet paper and detergent, but I get those at the dollar store.

All five trips cost me $181.38. That's less than I earned doing the three houses, so I'm still OK. My total in the tin box is now $1227.35.

I put all the food away and then I made orange cake. I also made lentil soup with carrots and cauliflower. Lentils are cheap and they give you a lot of protein and iron. Only the red lentils though. The green ones taste like mud.

I figured out that if I put newspaper at the bottom of the litter box I don't have to use as much litter. It's more work, because the newspaper gets all gross and has to be changed every day, but it's worth it. So now I have to start collecting old newspapers and plastic bags.

Yours forever,
Fern

Wednesday
November 28

Hi Xanoth,

I'm really depressed.

I called this place yesterday about a janitor job, and I was all excited because they said I should come over for an interview. The address was on Côte St. Luc Road, but all the way west, near the train tracks. It gets a bit slummy there, so I figured maybe I had a chance. I left really early, and the whole way on the bus I planned what I was going to say, like about being bilingual and having tools and knowing how to fix things. I was worried they'd test me by asking specific questions, but I figured with a bit of luck I'd be able to get away with it.

But when I saw the building I realized I didn't have a chance. It was at least twenty floors, and even though the area is bad, they fixed this building up. There was even a doorman.

I was going to turn back and go home, but right then an old lady came in and the doorman buzzed her through, so I went into the lobby with her. The doorman didn't stop me. He thought I was with the lady.

We got on the elevator and I pressed the third floor, which is where the office was. I figured I'd just peek in without telling them who I was.

The door of the office was open. There were lots of filing cabinets and computers inside, and a woman and a man were sitting behind two desks. They were the sort of people who basically want to be Barbies. They probably wake up every morning wishing their skin was made of plastic and their arms only moved in two directions.

I took the elevator back down and left the building. I had to wait forever for the bus, and there was this icy wind that goes right through to your bones. It was cold to begin with, but it was minus a zillion with that wind.

On top of everything, my nose was running because I was crying. I never cry where anyone can see me, but no one noticed or cared. It was too cold to notice anything.

Yours forever,
Fern

Saturday
December 8

Hi Xanoth,

I haven't written to you for a while because I've been kind of down. We had 31 cm of snow on Monday. A foot of snow doesn't sound like a lot, but it comes out to way more once you shovel it into piles. They said it was going to cost the city 17 million dollars to clean it up. I saw on TV how people were trying to dig out their cars.

Every year people act like they're surprised there's snow in Montreal.

Mostly I've been reading mysteries in bed, or lying on the sofa and watching videos from the library. Any old mystery video, including ones I've seen a hundred times, like Cracker or Death in Holy Orders. I also took out some travel videos, like Greece and Egypt, which I've also seen a zillion times. I'm not into depressing movies, or action movies, or horror, or comedies full of beautiful women and guys getting attracted to them, so that rules out a lot.

The only other thing I did was clean the Coopers' house on Wednesday.

Today I have some news though. I got a letter from Jack. The Coopers drove over this morning and put it in my mailbox. They also gave me a reference letter when I was there, but the way things are going I don't know if I'll ever need it.

Jack's letter goes,

Dear Fern, It was so heartwarming to hear from you but I am deeply grieved to hear about the passing of poor Felicity. She was a wonderful person and you were the light of her life. She loved you more than words can ever say and you will carry that love with you forever in your heart and remember it when you most need it. She sent me a photo of you when you were six and I've had it with me the whole time. You are beautiful inside and out, and I am sure you have grown up into a beautiful young woman.

I'm sure your friends and teachers at school are all there for you if you turn to them. I'm planning to come to Montreal but I don't know exactly when.

I had some dark times, but I'm on the right path now and listening to the good spirit inside me and letting it guide me. I'm enclosing twenty dollars for now. I'm sorry it isn't more.

Your loving uncle, Jack

Quite sappy, you have to admit. But at least he isn't a criminal type. I think he was in jail for stealing a car while he was drunk.

Xanoth, I don't know what to do next.

I'm thinking about your tulip and daffodil and pansy garden and about how flowers don't have seasons on your planet. They stay the same all year round. I love how when the sun sets the whole sky turns purple and gold and pink. I love how when it gets dark all the silvery lights come on and light up everything and people start dancing on the lawn in their flowing gowns. I love how people just go to stores and take what they want. How is Lulu? Will her wedding invitations have sparkles and rose petals on them, I wonder.

Yours forever,
Fern

Sunday
December 9

Hi Xanoth,

More news. Even though I figured it was hopeless, I've been checking the ads in the *Gazette* every day. Well, today I saw an ad that said SUPERINTENDENT IMME-DIATE 45 UNITS BILINGUAL REFERENCES. No tools and no experience, and they gave an address on Clanranald. There aren't any huge or expensive buildings there, I don't think, so I called and left a message.

Then I got impatient because no one was calling back, so I went down there to take a look at the place. I mean, I had nothing else to do and I thought at least I'd be able to see what kind of building it was. I had to buy a strip of six bus tickets, but I still have the Reduced Fare card from school, so I only paid $6.50 instead of $12.

It was unbelievably cold, and my ears almost froze off waiting for the bus and then looking for the building. Luckily there was a small space between the outside door and the buzzer door, so I went in and tried to thaw out a bit. The building's OK – five floors with an elevator, old but not too rundown.

One of the buzzers on the wall said JANITOR. I tried ringing it because I figured maybe the janitor who's leaving could tell me something about the job, but there wasn't any answer.

About half the mailboxes had names. In real dumps you never get more than one or two names, because the name either gets torn off or else the person's a criminal or junkie or doesn't know anyone, or just can't be bothered. Anyhow, who wants to visit you if you live in a dump? It's not like anyone's having Candlelight Suppers. That's from a show Mrs. Johnston liked, about a woman with illusions, and one of her illusions is that she's going to have all these candlelight suppers, whereas in reality everyone avoids her because she's insane. I got all excited around three years ago because I suddenly saw that video on the shelf in the library, and I remembered Mrs. Johnston talking about how she liked it, and how it showed that things on the outside don't count, only things on the inside. She laughed telling us about the show. I mean laughed almost out of control. We didn't really get what she was talking about, but it's always nice when your teacher's happy. It turned out to be a bit lame, but some parts were funny.

Anyhow, I was just about to leave the building when suddenly this man wearing a suit and a black coat came out of the elevator. He was around 30, not bad-looking. I could see he didn't live in the building. He was too well dressed and neat and in too much of a rush. He looked like a lawyer or someone important, but not fake like the Barbie people in that Côte St. Luc building. So I said, "Excuse me, do you know about the janitor job?"

He said in a big rush, "Yes, why?"

I could tell he was the person in charge, so I said, "I'd like to apply. I'm strong and I can fix anything. I have great references. And experience."

He looked surprised and very not sure. But he was in a huge rush, and that was my luck. He said, "How old are you?"

I told him I was nineteen but that I've been doing house-cleaning for three years. Which is true, actually. Apart from all the times Mom was sick, the summer Ricardo broke up with me I did a house on Old Orchard all on my own.

Well, the guy was really not sure, but because of his rush he said, "OK, come tomorrow at nine. No, make that ten." He handed me his card and hurried off. So at least I have an interview.

I was right, he's a lawyer. His name is David Frost. The only poem I know by heart is about frost.

> The door was shut, as doors should be,
> Before you went to bed last night,
> Yet Jack Frost has got in, you see,
> And left your window silver white.

I know all eight verses. Mrs. Johnston made us memorize that poem. Every day we memorized another verse, and when we knew the whole poem we got 20 bonus points.

I don't know if I even have a chance, Xanoth. Someone better could come along with more experience and with tools, or a couple. Also I'm not bilingual. I used to know French before Simone left, because until I was four we lived way out east where everyone was French. But I mostly forgot it after we moved.

Still, I don't think a janitor has to talk a lot. You can just fake it with "oui, oui" and "non" and pretend you know what the person's talking about. Besides, it's mostly immigrants on Clanranald. They don't know French either.

The good thing is that he told me to come in the morning, which means he probably won't see anyone between now and then. And maybe he's too busy to interview a lot of people. I'll bring the reference letter with me. The Coopers really exaggerated in that letter, but I'm not complaining.

I need this job, Xanoth. I never needed anything so badly.

Yours forever,
Fern

Monday
December 10

Hi Xanoth,

I had the interview today. I came at ten, but no one was there, so I waited an hour and a half in that little space. It was kind of claustrophobic, so I walked up and down in front of the building, but I only lasted a few minutes because it was freezing. There were some muddy flyers on the floor, and I picked them up and found a garbage pail to dump them in.

I was getting really stressed, thinking maybe I had the wrong time, or maybe David hired someone else and he couldn't call me because I didn't give him a phone number.

But finally he came rushing in. He was very impressed that I was still there.

He unlocked the buzzer door and we went into Apartment 101, on the ground floor. I guess that's the janitor's apartment. It's one room, with a kitchen area at one end and a bathroom at the other. There was a round table that had a weird black sort of cover, like something you'd put on a roof to keep out the rain.

We sat down at the table and he put his big briefcase in front of him and said again, "How old did you say you were?"

I said, "Nineteen. I was living with my mother, but she died. I'd be a really good janitor. I have a reference." I handed him the letter. I said, "It's from Dr. Cooper."

He said, "Dr. Cooper, who's that?" He talks like a lawyer.

I said, "I cleaned house for him and his wife. Only I haven't told them my mother died yet. I didn't want them to worry."

That was fast thinking, because imagine if he told them before I did. I realized I'd have to call and tell them as soon as I got home.

He read the letter, but he still looked suspicious. I said, "I'm really strong. I don't drink or smoke or anything. My church doesn't believe in it." I've never been to a church in my life, but I was desperate.

I could tell it was a good idea, mentioning a church. He relaxed a little and asked me my name, even though it was in the letter. He's a bit ADD, for a lawyer.

I said, "Fern Henderson. I used to help the janitor in our building, so I know what's involved. You could say I was his assistant."

He said, "Well, I was hoping for…" He didn't finish the sentence, probably because he knows all the discrimination laws. He was going to say he was hoping for a guy.

Then he said, "Well, here's the situation. My father owns this building but he's in the hospital, so I'm doing this for him for now, but I can't sign anything at this point." I could tell from the nervous way he said it that there are all sorts of complications with his father and the building.

I nodded. He told me the previous janitor quit, but there were three empty units and someone has to show them and keep an eye on the place and take out the garbage. But it would have to be a "casual arrangement" for now.

He gave me an application to fill in, which was a good sign. But then he said someone else was supposed to come for an interview, which got me all worried again.

He kept looking at his watch while I was filling in the form. He's cute, in a lawyer sort of way.

I remembered to change my date of birth on the form. A lawyer would notice right away. I gave Dr. Cooper's phone number for references.

Suddenly he remembered to ask, "Parles-tu français?"

I figured that's it for me, but by a miracle just as I was saying "Oui, oui" his phone rang and it was someone asking about the apartment. He was really annoyed. He tried not to show it and to answer all the questions, but his voice was all tense. He said they could come see the place on Saturday at two. He shut the phone and he was about to say something when it rang again.

This time the call was in French. It was about something else, private. Probably some case he's working on. He left the room to talk and when he came back he told me he had to run. He grabbed the paper and said, "I'm on the verge of a nervous breakdown."

Then he asked how soon I could start and I said right away.

So he said, "OK, I have a few more people who called for the job. If you don't hear from me by tomorrow evening it means I found someone else."

I think I have a good chance, Xanoth. Because think who else might apply. Some druggie or drunk. Or if it's a couple they might want a more reliable job, with a contract.

Also this guy doesn't have a lot of time to interview people. He wants to get it over with. And he believed me about the church. I'm also lucky he forgot about the French.

It's true I don't drink though. When I was going out with Ricardo we drank, but then after we broke up I wasn't interested anymore. Drinking would only make me think of him, and I'd feel like even more of a loser from loserland. I don't like drunk people anyhow. And smoking I promised Mrs. Johnston. I swear I think every kid in her class kept their promise on that.

When I got home I called the Coopers right away so I'd get to them before David. Mrs. Cooper answered.

I said, "Listen, I have to tell you something sad. My mom died of a heart attack."

She was really shocked. She kept saying oh no, oh no, how dreadful, I'm so sorry, what can we do, when's the funeral, etc. etc. I said there's no funeral because I donated her body and she said, "Oh you poor dear, would you like to come over?"

I said I couldn't right now because I was looking for work. I told her I was applying for a really great job to be the superintendent of a building on Clanranald and I gave their name for the reference. She said she'd give me a "glowing reference," and she made me promise to call with my new phone number if I got the job.

I said, "I didn't mention my age," and she understood right away and said, "Don't worry, I won't breathe a word about it." She probably doesn't know exactly how old I am.

I felt better after talking to her. At least she knew Mom.

Yours forever,
Fern

Tuesday
December 11

Hi Xanoth,

David called this afternoon. I was watching boring TV just to pass the time, and I jumped practically to the ceiling when the phone rang.

He said I got the job, and could I come over tonight for instructions. I didn't show how happy I was. I only asked when I should come, and he began muttering and mumbling and saying, "Hold on, hold on." I guess he was checking his appointment book. Finally he said, "Is eleven too late? It's just that I have a crazy day today."

I said, "No problem, Mr. Frost. I'll be there." He sounded relieved.

He was late as usual, this time by half an hour. He apologized a few times, but he wasn't really concentrating. He looked really tired and stressed.

We went into the apartment and he gave me printed sheets with information about the vacant units. He said he'll take the calls for the rest of the week, but if I could move in by Friday that would be great.

He said I have to keep the building clean and shovel the

snow out front and put salt down when it's icy. For the driveway a company comes with a machine. The driveway is where I put the garbage. The garbage has to be put out late on Monday and Thursday or before seven in the morning on Tuesday and Friday. I also have to show people the empty apartments, and if they're interested I have to give them an application form to fill in.

There's a secret code for the forms. I have to write 1 if I think the person looks OK, 2 if they're maybe OK, and 3 if they look like they're going to wreck the place and not pay. I'm not allowed to tell anyone about the code.

I also have to make sure everyone pays rent on the first of every month. There's a box in the hallway, and if they don't put their payment in the box I have to knock on their door. If I need to buy fuses or cleaning stuff or garbage bags I have to give David the receipt and he'll pay me back.

He showed me a cabinet with all the keys. It's in the coat closet of the apartment. Then he showed me where the fuse box was and I pretended I knew what it was.

The rent is free, along with heat and hot water and the phone, plus on top of that I get $200 a month. I really didn't expect that. But just as I was getting happy he said, "This is only a trial period. We'll see how it goes. Listen, if you find any files or papers let me know. My father's papers are missing."

Then he made me sign something about my responsibility if things got damaged in my apartment. He said, "Those people gave you a very good reference." He sounded like he was trying to convince himself that he wasn't making a mistake.

I said, "You'll be satisfied. I'm very reliable." He didn't look as if he trusted me, but he probably doesn't trust anyone.

So that's it. I have to move by Friday.

I'll miss this place. Our building's a dump, but the apartment is big – five rooms and a long hallway. And it has wood floors and a balcony in the back facing trees and a clothesline. I don't know how I'll fit our furniture into the new place.

Or how I'll move it all. I guess I'll have to call a mover from the newspaper.

I'm also worried about Beauty. She's going to miss having lots of rooms to prowl around in, and a balcony with trees to stare at.

I forgot to tell you, a letter came yesterday from McGill University. They thanked me for donating Mom's body and furthering science blah blah. They said I'll be invited to a ceremony in June to thank everyone who's donated a body, and there's also a monument at the Mont Royal Cemetery where they'll bury Mom when they finish with her, and I can go visit her there. I don't think I'll want to go to any sort of ceremony, but I called the number on the letter and gave them my new address, in case I change my mind. They caught me just in time.

Now I have to find my French dictionary and make sure I know how to say three rooms, heat and electricity included, $950.

Yours forever,
Fern

Wednesday
December 12

Hi Xanoth,

I took the bus down to Clanranald this morning to clean up the new apartment. I had to buy another strip of six tickets.

The apartment wasn't that dirty, actually. There are lots of cupboards in the kitchen part. The fridge is about a hundred years old, the kind you have to defrost, but it was clean too. I took the weird black roof cover off the table and put it in the equipment closet. You never know when you'll need something like that.

I also took the table and chairs down to the cellar. They aren't as nice as our table and chairs. Maybe at some point I can sell them for five or ten dollars.

When I finished cleaning, I went to the library and wrote down the phone numbers of a few movers from Saturday's *Gazette*.

At first I got into a huge panic, because everyone I called was saying $700 and $1000 for a move. And they were mean too, like they were angry at me for bothering them. That makes sense. Advertise your services, then yell at anyone who calls.

But finally there was one ad that said SMALL MOVES, AFFORDABLE. And the guy was normal. He didn't yell. He said if I had another person to help it would be $200. That was a lot cheaper than everyone else, plus he said he could come tomorrow morning, so I said OK.

I don't know how I'll fit all my furniture into one room. Actually, our place came furnished, so the furniture doesn't really belong to me, but I don't think the landlord remembers. What happened was that the old woman who lived here died. No one came to get her furniture, so when we rented the place the landlord raised the price from $400 unfurnished to $450 furnished. That's an extra $600 a year times ten years, plus all the rent hikes which would have been lower had we started off with $400. I think we've earned the furniture by now, especially since it didn't belong to the landlord in the first place.

Apart from the kitchen table and chairs, I have my bed, my night table, my bureau and attached mirror, Mom's double bed, her two bureaus, a sewing table, a cabinet with glass doors and a sofa.

The sofa I can leave behind. It's just junk by now. But everything else is made of nice dark wood.

I also want to keep Mom's belongings. The only thing I got rid of is her toothbrush, because it gave me the creeps. I couldn't get myself to throw it in the garbage, so I wrapped it and buried it. I've been collecting nice paper since I was a little kid, and I have a whole box full of pretty scraps. I chose a piece of light blue tissue paper to wrap around the toothbrush, and I buried it under some loose linoleum in the closet.

I'm going to miss this place a lot. We lived here a long time. Plus it's where I lived with Mom. Once I leave here, she'll really be gone from my life.

Yours forever,
Fern

Friday
December 14

Hi Xanoth,

I'm in my new apartment. I just woke up and remembered where I was. I must say I was happy that I have a safe place to live in. I took a long shower. It was weird using a different shower with different types of knobs.

Beauty can't figure out what's going on. She's going from corner to corner sniffing and meowing and making sure her food's still there.

The mover, Jeff, was nice. He has this old beat-up truck, and even though it was around minus 20 with the wind chill, all he had on was a sweater and a jean jacket. He thought for sure some guy would be there when he arrived. When I said it was only me, he laughed. I said, "I'm stronger than I look."

He didn't believe me at first, but when he saw how I lifted things he was impressed. The furniture's pretty heavy, but at least we didn't have to move the fridge and stove. The truck wasn't that big, so we had to make two trips. I had to put Beauty in a box. I had no choice. I'd kill myself if she got lost or run over. She was meowing like crazy.

Jeff laughed some more when he saw the size of the new apartment and what I was bringing into it, and he thought it was hilarious that I'm a janitor.

He said, "Hey, give me a call if you need any help. If I happen to be in the area, I'll drop by." He gave me his card, just like David. He lives in Verdun.

Before he left, we went down to the boiler room and he explained to me about fuses. It's not as hard as I thought. That was another thing he thought was funny, that I was the janitor and I didn't even know what fuses were. He took off his sweater because it was hot in the boiler room. He has a million tattoos. Some people are addicted to tattoos. I read about that in *Green Needle of Death*.

He didn't come on to me of course. That's one thing I don't have to worry about.

My new apartment looks like a storehouse now, but I like having all the furniture. I haven't finished unpacking, so it's still a mess, with boxes everywhere and no room to move. I have to climb over my bed to get from the bathroom to the kitchen.

I managed to take my bed apart before the move. The two boards are leaning against the wall. I didn't bother bringing my mattress because I'll be using Mom's. Jeff took my mattress and the sofa. He said he could use them in his basement and he took $20 off his price.

Julian came out while we were moving. He kept shouting, "Three months' notice, three months' notice," as if he's the landlord. How pathetic can you get? Like he hasn't been ranting about what a crook the landlord is for the past seven or eight years or however long he's lived in his stupid apartment. I ignored him. He tried to get out of me where I was moving to, but I basically told him to take a hike.

I was tired from the moving, but I wanted to clean the stairs, in case David came. The elevator means people don't use the stairs all that much, but they were still pretty dirty.

It was two in the morning by the time I finished. I had some tuna sandwiches and I passed out. For once I didn't have bad dreams.

Yours forever,
Fern

Saturday
December 15

Hi Xanoth,

I know there's no pain on your planet, but here on Earth
we have a lot of pain. The only thing you can do is take
drugs, but they don't always work. Today I got my period and I always get it bad. I saw a doctor about it once,
but she said the painkillers have side effects and the best
thing for me is to take Tylenol, which you can get gener-
ic for around $5.50 for 100.

I didn't have any period stuff left, so I took Mom's
bathrobe and cut it into pieces and I'm using that instead
of pads. I'm soaking the used ones in a pail, with a million soap bubbles so you can't see what's inside. Gross,
but who cares. That's what women must have done in the
old days, and probably still do in some countries.

I also took the last six Tylenols I had.

The phone rang nonstop about the empty apartments. I kept a neat list of names and phone numbers
and appointment times, so David can see I'm doing my
job. I managed OK with the French ones, don't ask me
how. Eleven people said they were going to come see the

apartments, but only four showed up. They all filled in application forms. I gave the first three a 1 rating, but I gave the fourth one a 3. I had bad vibes from him.

Apart from that, I lay in bed and moaned.

One problem with this apartment is that the TV doesn't work here. In our old place we managed to get two English channels without cable, but here all I can get is one blurry channel in French. I felt like smashing the stupid TV.

Yours forever,
Fern

Sunday
December 16

Hi Xanoth,

I had an idea. I remembered Ricardo's sister Michelle telling me about this clinic for teens, Head and Hands, that gives out free condoms. I'm hoping they also give free painkillers. I have to wait until tomorrow to call. They're closed on Sundays.

I'm worried that they'll be closed tomorrow too. We're having a blizzard again and they're predicting another 30 cm of snow. I went out to shovel about ten times, and each time it was like I was starting from scratch. Good thing the walkway is short.

I have to start thinking about a job with free food, but I can't concentrate. I didn't ask David if I'm allowed to have another job. If you don't ask you can say you didn't know.

Xanoth, I feel really down today. I hate this stupid tiny apartment. I hate that Mom died. How could she just die like that? Now I'll never have a chance to say goodbye or tell her I'm sorry.

Too bad I don't believe in God or heaven. Ginnie, a

girl I was once friends with, told me humans invented the idea of God millions of years ago to explain things like thunder and lightning.

Ginnie was the only girl I was ever friends with. That was in grade four, the same year I had Mrs. Johnston. She was in a different school, but she lived in the building next door. That building's a dump, but it tries to look like not a dump. They have a buzzer and a lobby and a laundry room in the basement, which we were allowed to use because the same company owns both buildings. They were more strict about who they rented to there.

Ginnie's apartment was smaller than ours, but it was in better shape. Ginnie had a sister who was three, and we used to babysit together when her parents went out. Grade four is kind of young to babysit, but all we had to do was stay awake and call Ginnie's parents on their cell if there was a problem.

Her parents were strange. The father was a nightclub singer and very old-fashioned. He was from France and he wore a suit and tie. The mom was very into looking sexy and having sexy underwear and perfume and done-up hair and low-cut sexy dresses. She always acted like she was in a play or a movie.

Ginnie was probably the nicest person I ever met. You don't usually get niceness like that in kids. She had a happy face and brown hair that was hard to brush because it was so curly. Everything she had, she wanted to share or give away. Even when her grandmother from

France sent her two hair clips with rhinestones, she gave me one.

I used to spend every weekend with her. On Saturday morning her parents made a special breakfast and they invited me. It wasn't really breakfast, because it was at noon, but they called it breakfast. They had marble cake and a lace tablecloth and blue candles in silver holders. Ginnie's dad said some prayer in another language and then they sang some of their old-fashioned nightclub songs in French. Ginnie and I wrote down the words of one of the songs, Ne Me Quitte Pas, and we sang it in the park at the top of our lungs, and everyone looked and we cracked up. I still remember the words. All the things I'll do for you if you don't go away.

Then all of a sudden in May, before school was even over, Ginnie's grandmother died and they moved to France to live in her apartment. Ginnie sent me two post-cards. I still have them. One's of the Eiffel Tower and one's of a statue. In the first one she gave me her address – Ginnie Sassoon, 147 rue de Sévigné, Paris 4ème. The year we were friends I wrote Fern Sassoon on all my books and notebooks. I forgot about that.

I thought of writing to her a few times, but she's probably got a million friends and barely remembers me. I only fit into her life because we were both little kids and I lived next door and she didn't know anyone else.

Anyhow, Ginnie's the one who told me God was invented. After that, I couldn't go back to believing. I only believed in the first place because of Simone. When I was little Simone told me about Adam and Eve and Jesus and Satan. But Ginnie said Adam and Eve couldn't be true because of evolution, and the stories about Jesus were made up a hundred years after he died, and Satan was like Dracula, just something that's meant to scare you. So that was it for me and God.

Xanoth, I'm trying to think about your planet, but I have to admit it's not working at the moment. My whole body from my waist to my knees hurts like hell.

This is so freaky – just as I was writing "hell" there was thunder and lightning! Right in the middle of a snow-storm! Maybe God didn't like what I was writing…

Yours forever,
Fern

Monday
December 17

Hi Xanoth,

I called Head and Hands this morning and told them my situation. They said I should come to the walk-in tonight. Usually the walk-in is on Tuesdays, but they're having an extra one this week because they'll be closed for the Christmas break.

They said it's a three-hour wait on average and they only take ten people, so I have to show up at least an hour early. My period isn't as bad today. The first two days are always the worst.

I thought maybe I'd walk there, but it's at least half an hour by foot, and it was minus 20 with the wind chill. So I took the metro to Vendôme and the 105 to the clinic.

The whole city is one big mess. Lots of sidewalks aren't cleared and you have to walk on the street or climb over huge mounds of snow. I don't know what old people are doing.

I was two hours early, so it was a long wait. I didn't mind. It was nice in the waiting room, with lots of magazines and old sofas and other kids who mostly looked even more messed up than me.

One girl was with her boyfriend. The whole time he

had his arm around her and she had her head on his chest. She had a million piercings – ears, eyebrows, lips, nose, tongue. It looked like overkill to me, but I guess her boyfriend liked them. I was jealous.

Everyone was very nice to me there. I told you Canada was a good country. I got free painkillers – a new kind that you take two days before your period's due. If the pills work, I can get more in three months. The nurse was funny. She wore this crazy hat with velvet flowers. Not what you'd expect a nurse to wear.

She also gave me a booklet that tells you where you can get help for different things. Reading the lists of all the services made me feel lucky that I didn't need them. Rape Crisis, Conjugal Violence, Immigrants, Bereaved Parents, Cancer Survivors, HIV, Colitis, Bipolar Disorder, Suicide Survivors... it goes on and on for pages.

They also have lists of things you can get cheap or for free, like free haircuts at a hairdressing school. I always cut my own hair though. I just chop off the ends when it gets too long. There's no point trying to do anything with your hair when it's as boring as mine. I used to cut Mom's hair too. She had nice hair, black and straight. My father was blond. Either one would have been good, but no such luck.

The nurse insisted on giving me some free condoms. What for? Even with Ricardo we didn't go all the way. But that's a whole other story.

Yours forever,
Fern

Tuesday
December 18

Hi Xanoth,

I spent the whole day cleaning the building. I even cleaned the elevator doors on all the floors and the glass of the buzzer door. Mom taught me a trick for cleaning glass with rolled-up newspapers.

There's an Asian family right opposite me on the ground floor. The kids are really adorable. I told the mom I could do babysitting in exchange for food, because they're probably too broke to pay me, and the smell of food coming from their apartment is really good.

She nodded and smiled, but I don't know if she understood me.

Yours forever,
Fern

Friday
December 21

Hi Xanoth,

Today David came over to get the application forms. He was impressed that I kept a good list of everyone who called and all the appointments. I also showed him how clean the place was.

David said it all looked great and then he asked me again if I'd come across any missing papers and files. He's very nervous about them being lost.

I said maybe they're in a safety deposit box, but he made this sarcastic sound and said, "That'll be the day." I don't think he gets along with his father.

Luckily Beauty was hiding under the bed. Pets aren't allowed in the building.

After he left I noticed I was running out of toothpaste. I remembered when I was a kid, they always gave us a free toothbrush and a little tube of toothpaste at the dentist's. So today I walked all the way to Côte des Neiges, to the building we used to go to. It was minus nine, but at least it wasn't too windy. I have thermal socks and a huge mohair scarf, both of which I found at a vestiaire.

Sometimes you get lucky at those places. My coat sucks though. It weighs a ton and isn't even that warm, but it's all I could find in my size.

The building on Côte des Neiges is full of dentists. I went into the first office I saw, and asked for a toothpaste sample. I said it was for a project on teeth at my school. The receptionist gave me two different brands plus a toothbrush.

I was going to leave, but then I figured if I had luck at one office, maybe I can try some others. So I got a plastic bag from the pharmacy downstairs, and I went from office to office asking for toothpaste. Some receptionists were real bitches and looked at me as if I had a contagious skin disease, but most were OK.

I now have enough toothpaste for five years, and enough toothbrushes for the rest of my life.

Yours forever,
Fern

Saturday
December 22

Hi Xanoth,

I finished putting everything away. I stacked six boxes in the equipment closet with Mom's purse, her wallet, her dresses, her jeans and her belts. Simone and I chose her dresses for her when we went to Value Village. She wouldn't have bought them by herself, but I liked dressing her up, especially when I was a little kid.

The belts were the only thing she bought on her own. She liked wearing carved or braided belts with interesting buckles in front.

I felt horrible folding her clothes and putting them in the boxes. I didn't even think it was possible to feel so horrible and sad. There were like a hundred levels of sadness and they all joined together at the same time. I kept thinking Mom was standing behind me watching me, and I even had to turn around a few times to make sure. I was crying my eyes out. I remembered how we played Mille Bornes and how she didn't want to give me the obstacle cards and it made me feel like I was shriveling up and dying.

I remember exactly the day I started being mean to her. It was when Ricardo broke up with me. I got home and Mom asked, "How was your day?" and I just got so mad at her suddenly. I screamed, "Get away from me," and I went to my room and slammed the door.

I guess you're wondering about Ricardo. I met him in the park. He went to Sunnyview, but I never noticed him in school.

It was the beginning of May and really warm, and I was sitting on the bench with a bag of chips, getting some air. Then out of nowhere, Ricardo came over.

I thought he was going to ask for something, like a light or some chips, but he said, "Why you be chillin here alone, girl?" I ignored him. I figured he was probably either stoned out of his mind or else he thought I was a hooker.

But he sat down next to me on the bench. We were sitting there not talking when an old guy walked by with his poodle. This poodle was really tiny, like a puppy, but he began barking at us as if he thought he was some kind of huge ferocious guard dog. The old guy was walking really slowly, so the poodle had a lot of time to bark, and we started laughing.

Somehow that broke the ice and we got talking. Ricardo said he liked dogs, but his older sister Michelle liked cats, so they never got a pet. I began telling him about Beauty and why cats are good pets. I convinced him, and he said he'd get Michelle a kitten for her birthday. The next thing you knew, he invited me over to his place.

There are a lot of things I still don't get. Like why he went out with me.

I knew it wasn't a dare or anything, because his sister Michelle told me it wasn't, and she was into feminism. She had all these posters and buttons saying WOMYN POWER. She'd know if he was lying.

So maybe some people are just weird. Like you hear about guys who like all kinds of messed-up things that you wouldn't believe could turn anyone on.

In school we only said hi, and on Sundays Ricardo worked at Wendy's, but we got together on Saturday and Saturday night.

He was a bit bad, but not too much. We got drunk, and once we threw bottles at a wall in an alley and we wrote graffiti, but that was about it. We went to Old Montreal mostly. Old Montreal is cool. We used to go there with Simone when I was a kid. It has ancient buildings from when the explorers first came and ancient cobblestone streets. When the weather's nice everyone sits out in cafés and you can watch artists on the street drawing people. They have horse rides too, for tourists. I always felt sorry for those horses. They didn't look too happy, trapped inside all those harnesses.

Ricardo told me a lot about his life. He had leukemia for two years when he was around eleven. His dad was a bus driver and his mom was a nutritionist who went to schools and told kids how to eat better. His grandparents also lived with them.

We made out in my room. He didn't want to go all the way because of a dream he had when he was in the hospital with leukemia. He was getting a lot of transfusions and they gave him nightmares, or maybe it was the drugs, and he had a bad dream about sex. He dreamed he saw someone doing it, and their dick came off and stayed inside the woman, and he woke up feeling sick. I knew what he meant, because I've had dreams where my teeth fall out.

I almost began to think I wasn't totally repulsive, with Ricardo. He used to say, "This is the best part of my week by far, girl."

He was good at comedy. That's what I really liked about him, how funny he could be. He didn't just copy jokes from TV. He made them up as he went along. Like we might pass some old man and he might start pretending to be that old man and saying in an old man's voice, "Laddy, in my day we didn't even have wheels. We just rolled people up. Never did work too good." It was more the crazy way he said it.

He got along OK with Michelle and his dad but not with his mom. She was always after him to do better in school. His mother's name was Angela, but he called her Lady Jane. Sometimes she'd say, "Don't you Lady Jane me, young man," but she didn't really mind.

Then two weeks after school ended, he broke up with

me. Not that I was surprised or anything. It was a fluke all along. He said he met some other girl who worked at Wendy's, and that was it.

That's when I started being mean to Mom. And believe me, Xanoth, Mom never did a thing to deserve it. She never raised her voice in her life. That's because of what she went through when she was a kid, on the farm.

Apart from ignoring her, I began to snort at everything she said as if it was the stupidest thing I ever heard in my life. She'd start telling me about something from the past and I'd give this huge yawn. So she stopped, and then she had no one to talk to. And I lost out too, because she used to brush my hair at night, and now I wouldn't let her near me.

It was the worst summer. I was so desperate to take my mind off things that I got something in the park. I don't know what it was, but it was a total waste of money and it only made me feel a million times worse. First I thought I was being chased by the cars on the street. I knew I wasn't, but I couldn't get rid of the feeling that they were all after me.

Then I thought these zombie-like ghouls were walking next to me. That totally freaked me out.

Then when I got into bed I shut my eyes and these scenes began flashing through my mind. I never even knew I had scenes like that in me. Like horrible car accidents, or this giant guillotine that terrorists were using to kill a thousand people at a time. It was sick.

I had these scenes three nights in a row, but they were shorter and more faded the second and third night. So that was my first and last time with drugs. I don't know if it was a cheapo rip-off drug, or if that's just the way drugs affect some people.

Anyhow, that was my summer. Mom had a house back then on Old Orchard that I pretty much took over, so at least I made some money. I couldn't stand the people who lived in that house, but I didn't have to see them much. The father was in politics and the mother thought she was an artist but her stuff sucked. All she did was glue strips of metal on a canvas. Every single thing in their house was ugly, like metal masks and metal everything. And the two boys were thieves. Their parents had to pick them up from the station for stealing CDs from the Bay.

Yours forever,
Fern

Sunday
December 23

Hi Xanoth,

David signed two new leases – one with a student from Germany, and the other with three girls. The German guy shook hands with me as if I was an important person. I guess people are more polite in Germany. The girls are really giggly and young, around nineteen, and David didn't think they'd be reliable, but he agreed to take them.

That leaves one more apartment. I hope it gets rented soon. It's tiring answering the phone and making appointments and then people don't show up, or they do show up and I have to take them around. They ask such stupid questions sometimes, like "Do you get noise from the street here?" With the cars going right below! No, that's just an illusion you're having. There is no noise here at all because actually we're in a castle on the hills of Scotland. It only looks like an apartment building on Clanranald near Queen Mary.

I got really depressed again today, Xanoth. Beauty doesn't like this place. This morning I let her out in the hallway while I was washing the floor because I know she'd never run out if someone came in. She's too scared of strangers.

I was right. She stayed next to me the whole time. She kept sniffing the pail of water, but luckily she didn't put her paw in. The smell of the detergent was too strong.

I had to buy more food. There's a Provigo on Monkland and it got really warm suddenly, so it wasn't a problem walking there. It was actually raining.

At the check-out I began talking with the cashier about how expensive the fruits and vegetables were, and she actually told me about this store on Somerled that sells them for a lot less! She'd probably get fired if they knew she's sending customers somewhere else.

I found the store and she was right. The prices were way lower for fruits and vegetables. Which is good, because I was having a craving for fresh food.

Everything together cost me $204.14. It didn't make sense to make a lot of trips if I'm paying for bus tickets, so I asked for delivery and walked home.

I really need to get a job with free food, Xanoth. There's a retired guy on the first floor who gets the *Gazette* every day, and he doesn't come out for it until around noon, so I borrowed it yesterday to check the ads for hotel kitchens and restaurants. I called a few places, but so far nothing. Mostly they want cooks.

The system here with the garbage is a disaster. Tenants are allowed to stick their garbage in pails at the end of the driveway, and then I'm supposed to take them out front in time for the pick-up on Tuesdays and Fridays.

The problem is that some of the tenants want to save on garbage bags, so they put their garbage in stupid little grocery bags which I have to dig out and put in regular garbage bags. There was a whole stack of super-strong garbage bags under the sink in my apartment. Now I know why.

Another problem is that there isn't enough room in the pails, and the whole area is a huge disgusting mess.

I decided to make signs with new rules. I made six bilingual signs. One of the tenants, Louise, helped me with the French. I taped them all over the building with black tape from the tool box. The sign says:

NEW GARBAGE POLICY. TENANTS ARE ALLOWED TO BRING DOWN THEIR GARBAGE ONLY ON MONDAYS AND THURSDAYS AFTER 6:00 P.M. ALL GARBAGE HAS TO BE IN LARGE GREEN BAGS OR IT WILL BE RETURNED TO THE TENANT. THANK YOU FOR YOUR COOPERATION. THE MANAGEMENT.

I couldn't believe I wrote that sign. It's like you see signs like that all your life, and you think you're ignoring them, but they're going into your brain. Like signing THE MANAGEMENT. I didn't even know I knew that word.

Yours forever,
Fern

Monday
December 24

Merry Christmas, Xanoth,

I got a card with forty dollars from Jack, c/o the Coopers. They mailed it to me along with their own card and a pair of really nice suede mitts.

I'll send Jack a card back and give him this address. Simone left behind a set of 50 Christmas cards and there are still about ten left.

Actually, I should write to Simone and tell her about Mom, but I don't really feel like it. Every Christmas she sends us one of those Letters to Everybody, so I know she married a widower with diabetes and three kids, and they had another kid together. I don't know the latest, because I stopped reading her letters a while back. *Here we all are tobogganing in the snow and having fun.* Now I can die.

The way Mom met Simone was she had a ride from Manitoba to Montreal, and she stopped at a store to pick up a few things, and there was Simone's notice on the wall, APARTMENT TO SHARE.

Simone was around 30 with blond hair to her shoulders. She was a massage therapist at the Y. She talked and laughed pretty much non-stop.

Simone knew a million things about how to get stuff. She knew about Value Village and the vestiaires and where you could go for picnics. We used to go to Île Ste-Hélène in the summer and we'd spread out a blanket and eat hard-boiled eggs and cookies. Simone always treated me to ice cream. She said two scoops was best, because three were hard to manage and one was boring. She liked doing nails and toes. She shampooed my hair in the bath and made me French braids.

Simone taught Mom how to cook. She found this one recipe in a magazine where you fry chopped onions and tomatoes and green peppers and then when they're almost ready you break four eggs on top and cover the frying pan tight and the eggs get done from the steam. The trick is not to break the yolks when you crack the eggs into the pan. Simone had a food processor, so the chopping only took a few seconds, on off on off on off, to get it even. We made that recipe a lot.

Simone saved us, because Mom didn't know where to get clothes or anything else.

When I was seven, Simone decided to move to Kitchener, where she had some friends. At first I thought she was moving to a new job in a *kitchen*, but eventually I figured out that she was leaving Montreal. She said it was easier to do massages in Ontario.

We couldn't afford the apartment without Simone, so

we had to move. Before she left, Simone helped us find a new place. Come to think of it, she's the one who bargained with the landlord about keeping the old woman's furniture. Unfortunately, she took her food processor when she left. A lot of those recipes weren't the same without it.

That's all I have to tell you about today.

There were two cards for the janitor who lived here before me. I took them out of the envelopes and put them next to my cards. They're both in Spanish.

Yours forever,
Fern

Wednesday
December 26

Hi Xanoth,

There was a noise problem last night. There's an oboe player on the third floor, and his playing bothers this East Indian guy under him who has to work early and is trying to get some sleep.

I'm going to ask David if the oboe player can move to the apartment on the top floor in the corner, which is still empty. It's the same size and rent. The people under that apartment don't look like the type to complain. They're a guy and girl, around 20, very cool and into themselves. They act like they're living in New York and hanging out with rock stars. They'll like having a black oboe player living on top of them. It will help them with their illusions.

Yours forever,
Fern

Monday
Midnight December 31

Hi Xanoth,

Happy New Year.

Yours forever,
Fern

Wednesday
January 2

Hi Xanoth,

We got another 20 cm of snow dumped on us.

David came by to pick up the latest applications. I talked to him about Victor, the oboe guy. David said it's fine with him, but he didn't think Victor would want to get a new phone, because Bell charges an arm and a leg for a move. I didn't think of that.

He said, "What I really need is the original copy of the lease but I can't find those bloody leases or anything else." He looked like he was ready to kill someone. Then his phone rang and he had to run off.

I went to tell Victor. He said he doesn't have a landline and he doesn't mind moving to another apartment, as long as it's a three and a half. He said, "I need space for my body and soul."

He told me a bit about himself. He used to play in an orchestra, but then he got divorced and missed rehearsals, so now he plays in a fancy club four nights a week. He has two kids. I was surprised about that. He doesn't look the type. He says he doesn't see them much. He wants to, but his wife doesn't want him in her life. She has a new guy and they live in Beauharnois, wherever that is.

I got a peek at his apartment. His mattress is on the floor, covered with a cozy red wool blanket, and he has lots of CDs. There was a definite smell of ganja.

I told him I'd help him move in exchange for a meal and he said, "Cool."

I felt a bit down after I talked to him. Because I liked him, and I knew that someone like him would never in a million years go for someone like me.

At least I have you, Xanoth.

Yours forever,
Fern

Thursday
January 3

Hi Xanoth,

I helped Victor move his stuff today. He didn't have all that much, and nothing was really heavy. He was nice, cracking jokes and worrying about me when we were carrying his bureau up the stairs. He called me Miss Hercules.

He wanted to give me a CD of his playing, but I told him I don't have a CD player. He said I should come over some time to listen to it.

He forgot about the meal, or maybe he thought I was joking when I told him we'd do an exchange. So I reminded him. I said, "Well, you owe me a meal."

He laughed and said, "Any time, honey."

What does that mean?

Yours forever,
Fern

Friday
January 4

Hi, Xanoth,

Mrs. Cooper called to wish me Happy New Year. She invited me for dinner tomorrow. I couldn't think of an excuse, so I had to say yes. Then she asked if there was anything I didn't like, and I said, "I don't eat mammals." She laughed and said, "Okey-dokey, no mammals. Is spinach lasagna OK?"

I was surprised to hear Mrs. Cooper laugh.

Yours forever,
Fern

Sunday
January 6

Hi Xanoth,

I finally found an ad for kitchen help that didn't say EXPERIENCE. I have an interview tomorrow morning in Park Extension. I never even heard of Park Extension. I'll ask at the metro how to get there.

Dinner at the Coopers was OK. They invited another couple with a son called Paul who's around 16. They mostly talked about computers and how they're affecting the world, and Paul explained iPods to them. He's very cute. Totally out of my league.

Then they asked me what I'm doing and I said I was a janitor, and they acted like I got chosen to go up in space.

I mentioned Beauty, and that led to a long discussion of pets. The Coopers talked about experiences they had with animals in Africa. Mrs. Cooper's allergic to cats.

The food was OK. The lasagna was a bit soggy but I liked the salad and there was very good cheesecake for dessert. There was wine too, but I didn't have any. I was afraid it might affect me in a stupid way and I'd ruin whatever credit I'd managed to get with them.

After dinner Paul played songs from Broadway shows on the piano. The Coopers kept saying how talented he was.

Paul asked me if I had any requests. Out of the blue, I remembered one of the sappy songs Ginnie's parents sang on Saturdays. I told Paul how the chorus went and he knew it. Mais mon amour... He didn't know the words, but he knew the tune, and he made up funny words in English. Like oh you my friend, you have such nice new clothes from Gap, my friend. I'll give you everything I own, my friend, for that nice T-shirt.

Paul's parents gave me a lift home. The windshield kept fogging up because their fog thing wasn't working right, so I had to wipe the glass in front and Paul kept wiping the side windows. We both used our sleeves. When we got to my place they said, "It was a pleasure meeting you. We must do this again."

They were just saying it, but that's OK.

Yours forever,
Fern

Monday
January 7

Hi Xanoth,

I got hired at a Lebanese restaurant!

I get $50 cash for the evening, six to midnight, with a half hour break in the middle to eat, and I get paid every Sunday. On Mondays they're closed. The good thing is that it's evenings, in case David comes to check on things during the day. Another good thing is that the restaurant is two blocks from the Jean Talon metro. That means I don't have to take any buses, and the metro ride is only eight stops.

The woman who interviewed me was wearing a bright red dress and about thirty silver bracelets. I brought the reference letter from Dr. Cooper and she read it with this paranoid look on her face. Then she turned the letter around to see if something was written on the back. She did that like ten times.

I was sure I wouldn't get the job, but she said I could start tomorrow. Her name is Mrs. Taza, and she and her husband own the restaurant. She said supper was included, but I can only eat certain foods that aren't going fast.

They get to decide. I said right away that anything was fine with me and that I don't eat beef or lamb or pork. I could tell she was glad to hear that.

What I'm hoping is that I can take home all the food they're planning to throw out. But maybe Mrs. Taza takes the leftovers home herself. I'll see how it goes. At least I'll get experience.

I had to buy a bus pass for January. It's $36 with my Reduced Fare card, which doesn't expire until the summer. That leaves me with one bus ticket I don't need. Maybe I can sell it to the giggly girls on the third floor. They're probably not eligible for reduced fare, so it's a saving for them.

Yours forever,
Fern

Tuesday
January 8

Hi Xanoth,

The building is falling apart!!!!

I got a call really early this morning from the East Indian guy on the second floor. He said one of the bathroom pipes is leaking and it flooded the floor and the water's dripping into the bathroom in the apartment below. Then all of a sudden everyone was calling me about water problems, like their hot water only comes out in a gush or not at all and their toilet is leaking and taps aren't closing.

I pretended I wasn't in a total panic. I called the guy who moved me, Jeff, on his cell and asked him what to do. He said he was going to be in the area and he'd come by at noon.

I was a mental case until he showed up. On top of everything else, I was worried because I had to leave for the restaurant at five. I took Jeff to see the problem apartments. He said it's a job for a plumber, and no one expects me to be a plumber. He said the pipes have to be replaced.

He came on to me. I guess he's one of those guys who doesn't care what you look like. They just want sex bad. I said I was too stressed out and maybe another time. I don't think he was serious anyhow.

I called David and luckily he came over right away. He swore under his breath and began making these angry calls on his cell, some of them in French, all about money and who's going to pay for what. I told you there were big problems with who owns the building.

I got from the conversation that David's father is unconscious and they need him to sign over the power or something like that. Meanwhile he's not dead but he's not conscious so that's the problem, but it's more complicated.

Finally David said a plumber would be coming first thing tomorrow. He was in the worst mood. He didn't take it out on me though. Actually, he sort of joked. He said, "Well, Fern, I hope you can swim."

Gotta run!

1:45 a.m.

My job was a nightmare. The guy in charge, Amir, is severely communication disabled. He'll say DISHES and I'm supposed to figure out if that means wash the dishes, dry the dishes, put food on the dishes, or what. Or FILL POT and he doesn't bother saying fill with what or how much. Or PUT IN MICROWAVE. I never used a microwave in my life. He's around 30 and his English is fine. He just has a communication problem. Or maybe a personality problem.

There's another cook who's very good-looking and much friendlier. I didn't catch his name. He didn't say a word to me all evening, but in his case I think he really doesn't know much English.

The owners do the cash. The paranoid wife does some of the waitressing if it gets busy, but the main waitress is a skinny pretty redhead, around 20. To someone like that someone like me is invisible.

I was sure I'd get fired after tonight. It wasn't my fault. I can't read minds. But they didn't say anything. I was there until one. The job ended at midnight and they told me I could leave, but I still had more pots to wash and I didn't want to leave a mess on top of everything else I did wrong.

The only good thing was supper. The food was weird, and I was afraid I wouldn't like it, but I did. They didn't watch to see how much I was eating. Amir kept going in and out of the kitchen, Mr. and Mrs. Taza don't come in the back, and the quiet guy doesn't care what I do. I had pita with fried chicken, rice with vegetables, rice with lentils, rice with chickpeas, fried potatoes, fried cauliflower, bean salad, and falafel, which I heard of but never tasted before. So at least that part went OK, but they'll probably fire me by the end of the week.

The place was full most of the evening. A lot of people can afford to eat out. Or else they can't afford it but they use their credit card.

I'm in bed now. I like sleeping in Mom's double bed. My old bed was a single and the mattress was saggy, but Mom's is still OK.

Yours forever,
Fern

Wednesday
January 9

Hi Xanoth,

My arms are killing me from lifting those heavy pots yesterday. The Tazas haven't called to fire me, so I guess I'm working again tonight. They probably couldn't find anyone to replace me on such short notice. At least I'll make another $50.

The plumbers were here all day, and tomorrow some builders are coming to repair the damaged floors and ceilings.

I had a conversation in the hallway with this woman who lives on the fourth floor. She's around 35, kind of high strung, with really bad taste in clothes, like a top with vinyl pink hearts, and tight white slacks with a metal belt, and high heels with sequins. Her name's Adorée and she has an eight-year-old daughter. I really like that name – Adorée. She told me she had her daughter with a man who's been coming to see her almost every evening and on weekend afternoons for 16 years, even though he a wife and three kids at home. And his wife doesn't know a thing about it! He tells his wife he's working late, or that he has to go to the office on the weekend to catch up, and he never lets her see how much he makes so she doesn't know that he gives Adorée a big part of his money. He runs his own import company, so I guess he makes enough for his wife and for Adorée.

I can't believe his wife doesn't know. How can you not slip up in 16 years? I mean, how clued out can a person be? Also, if Adorée goes around telling people, wouldn't someone eventually tell his wife? But Adorée said his wife has no idea at all.

I read a murder mystery once about a guy like that. He ended up in a cement mixer.

Yours forever,
Fern

Thursday
January 10

Hi Xanoth,

The restaurant job was a little better yesterday. I only made about a thousand mistakes. I also managed to fill a plastic bag with scraps for Beauty. Instead of scraping food that people left on their plates into the garbage, I scraped some of it into a plastic bag to take home. Beauty couldn't believe her luck when I filled her plate with chicken. I have enough for a week at least.

New tenants moved into the last vacant apartment today – an old pruny woman and her son. I have a bad feeling about her. I gave them a 1 because I was sure they'd pay, but now I think maybe I should have given them a 3. I think I was just getting tired of showing the apartment. It's the one where Victor lived before he moved upstairs.

The woman's name is Mrs. Coleville. Her son, who's around 30, is called Markus. Markus looks exactly like Humpty Dumpty. He never says anything. He just stands quietly next to his mother but half a step back, as if he's a kid who got sent to the corner, except that the corner for him is behind his mother's shoulder.

The reason I'm worried about Mrs. Coleville is all the complaining she's been doing. She says everything needs repairs in her apartment. She gets really angry, and she acts like everyone's her servant. You should have seen the way she shouted at the movers. You wouldn't think such an old skinny person could have such a loud bossy voice. All that's missing is a rifle on her shoulder and a whistle.

The rent in this building is really high, considering how rundown it is. It's $850 for a two and a half, $950 for a three and a half and $1025 for a four and a half. That's why they'll be glad we left our old place. They'll double the rent now.

On her application form Mrs. Coleville wrote that her former address was in Beaconsfield, and she was a home-owner for 38 years.

Those houses in Beaconsfield are mansions. Mom used to clean a place out there, but I made her quit because she had to take two buses and a train, and they wouldn't even pay for the train.

I wonder how you can go from a mansion to this place in like one month? Especially a three and a half for two people. Markus will have to sleep in the living room.

Everyone else in the building is OK, I think. Some of the tenants are a bit grumpy, but they're not a problem. But Mrs. Coleville has a long list of complaints: the windows are stuck, there's paint on the glass, the linoleum in the kitchen has cracks, the bathroom mirror is stained, those wood strips between the floor and the wall are coming off in a few places, the bedroom lock is broken, and I forget what else. She made it sound like everything that's gone wrong in her life is my fault and I have to fix it.

I told her I'd talk to David, but he's just going to say that this is what you get for $950.

I really wish I'd given her a 3!

Yours forever,
Fern

Monday
January 14

Hi Xanoth,

It's my day off. I baked two cakes and slept most of the day.

The restaurant job is a bit better. I don't think they'll fire me. Amir is still not explaining anything, but I can mostly figure out what he wants me to do.

So now I have my supper taken care of. But I need more food, and I need to make more than $50 a day. That means I'm going to have to find a job for during the day at a hotel or restaurant.

Mrs. Coleville is driving me crazy. I really made a mistake with her. She left like twenty messages on my machine while I was at the restaurant, asking where I was and complaining that the door of the woman next to her keeps banging all night.

Then this morning she woke me up at eight. I'm a deep sleeper, but she was pounding away on my door. Beauty got totally freaked out.

I crawled out of bed and opened the door. She didn't care that she woke me up. She was probably happy about it. She stood there in the hallway, with Markus in his usual spot. She began ranting again about people going in and out of the apartment next to her all night. She said, "I'm paying enough rent. I expect decent accommodations, not a house of ill repute." She has a kind of British accent. Fake, if you ask me.

I left a message for David. He called back a few minutes later, and I told him there was a problem with one of the tenants. I said she's been asking for repairs and she's complaining about doors banging.

He asked, "What kind of repairs?" in that lawyer's voice that's sort of scary. I told him the list and he said what I thought he'd say – "I guess she thinks this is a luxury condo." Then he sighed and said, "Well, do what you can. Next time I'm there I'll take a look."

Yours forever,
Fern

Monday
January 28

Hi Xanoth,

I haven't written in a while because I get home late and then when I get up I have to clean the building and shovel and pick up the flyers and deal with Mrs. Coleville. I found some glue in the tool box and I glued the loose strips in her apartment. I also scraped the paint off the windows with a knife. I can't fix anything else. I can't put in new windows or new linoleum or replace the bathroom mirror. I promised her the owner would look in, but David hasn't been here since I told him.

She's still going on about the banging door. I promised to talk to the tenant. She's this mousy woman who reminds me of the war refugees in *Murder Without Borders*, with her big winter coat and rubber boots. A Value Village shopper like me, but with weird taste.

Mrs. Coleville also expects me to shovel every five minutes when it starts snowing. It snowed the entire day last Tuesday, and I went out to shovel three or four times before I went to work, but she complained that I wasn't there to shovel in the evening. What makes it so annoying is that she doesn't even go out.

I should feel sorry for Mrs. Coleville, but I don't. Adorée found out from Markus that her husband sold the house in Beaconsfield while she was out shopping. He did the whole thing secretly. Then he took all the money and vanished. He took all her jewels too. The only thing he left was the furniture, and that's what she's living on – money she made from selling most of the stuff in the house.

Well, all this could explain why Mrs. Coleville is so mad, but it doesn't explain why she acts like everyone around her is a cockroach she can squash with her shoe. Or why she keeps pounding on my door like a mental case every morning and leaving me a million messages when I'm not home, as if my whole purpose in life is to stay in my apartment and wait for her next rant.

Another thing I'm worried about is Beauty. I feel bad leaving her alone so much. She really misses her old life, with all the rooms and the balcony and a view of trees.

Maybe I can leave her with Victor. He mentioned he likes cats, and he's home during the day, and his place is a lot bigger than mine.

One thing about working, it keeps your mind off things. You fall into bed and the next thing you know it's time to get up and clean.

I've been reading the ads in the retired man's *Gazette*, but so far the restaurants are all too far or the wrong hours, and I only saw two hotel ads, one for valet parking and one for bartending.

I'm wearing my second-to-biggest jeans now, which I haven't worn in a long time. It's from all the running around, and having less time to eat, or even to buy food.

Yours forever,
Fern

Tuesday
January 29

Hi Xanoth,

Mrs. Coleville and I are having a contest. It's called "Who's going to go over the edge first?" She's been writing down every single time the door of the mousy woman opens and closes.

Meanwhile I've been trying to talk to the mousy woman, because I really would like to sleep in now and then instead of being yelled at by Mrs. Coleville while I'm half-conscious.

But the mousy woman has a peephole, and when she sees it's me she doesn't answer. And I don't start pounding away because I'm not Mrs. Coleville. Yet.

Yours forever,
Fern

Wednesday
January 30

Hi Xanoth,

I finally talked to the mousy woman. She came in with groceries while I was doing the floors. She was soaking wet. It's been half-raining, half-snowing most of the day.

I said, "I'm sorry to bother you, but the tenant next door to you is very sensitive to noise. She hears every time your door opens and closes, especially at night."

The mousy woman looked scared. She has a wide pale face with big pale blue eyes. "I more quiet," she said with an accent. Her accent might explain her refugee coat and rubber boots. Maybe she really is a refugee.

I hope I'll be able to sleep in the mornings now, without that Coleville maniac trying to kick my door in.

Yours forever,
Fern

Sunday
February 10

Hi Xanoth,

This morning I found an ad for a hotel job that looked good. It said CLEANING AND GENERAL HELP and it also said IMMEDIATE, which brought me luck last time. I think it means they're desperate.

So I called and a guy answered. He said, "Just to tell you right off, we're in the gay village." Kind of random, but I said OK. He wanted me to come over right away and he gave me directions. So I left a note on my door – BACK SOON – mostly so Mrs. Coleville won't have a fit.

On the phone the man told me the hotel was very easy to find, but I almost missed it. I imagined a big hotel, but it was a plain low-rise and kind of old, so I went right past it without seeing the sign. It's called Le Baudelaire.

I went in and told the receptionist who I was. He had a purple punk hairdo, but the rest of him wasn't punk at all. He was dressed like he was in an ad for sailing. So that was weird and the building was weird, and for a second I thought maybe it's a trap, like in one of those urban legends where they pretend there's a job and then they kidnap you and take out your kidney or sell you into slavery.

But I relaxed when he said, "Wonderful, wonderful." He sounded normal. A second guy heard us and came out from his office and shook my hand.

The second guy seemed kind of lost, around 40, with thin messy hair. His office was a mess too. He kept looking for something on his desk, only he couldn't remember what he was looking for.

He told me the hotel catered mostly to gays and he was telling me right out front that some of the customers are probably or for sure HIV and the pay is minimum wage, which is $8.00. It's 3 hours during the week and 5 hours on Saturday and Sunday.

He told me that even though he's the owner he does some of the housekeeping himself, but he can't manage alone. He needs someone to fix rooms, keep the place clean, and help a person called Sally with laundry.

He said he wants someone stable who'll stay and not vanish, because he had three people in a row who vanished without notice. He said the hours were flexible. Check-out time is 12:00 and check-in time is 4:00, so I can show up any time between 12:00 and 2:00. I said I'd need Mondays off. That's the day I get off at the restaurant, and I need a free day to catch up on shopping and sleep and bake cakes for the week. He said that was fine, especially since Mondays are slow anyhow.

I asked if they had a kitchen. He said yes, but it's only

to store beverages and sandwiches and so on. They don't cook or anything like that.

So I asked if lunch was included, and right away he got this nervous look on his face and said people bring their own lunch.

I was afraid I'd blown it, so I said quickly, "I'm definitely interested." The hours are perfect, and even if lunch isn't included, I can probably get shampoo and soap and maybe toilet paper. Also, I've been getting more food from the restaurant lately. They let me fill a styrofoam take-home container every night, and I can take as much pita as I want. They have huge bags of pita in their freezer.

He relaxed and said, "Are you sure you want it?" He didn't mean am I sure I'm going to show up and stick to it. He meant am I sure I want such a bad job.

I don't know why he thinks it's bad. Anywhere you work, people might have HIV or a million other diseases, including weird ones from distant countries, like bird flu or SARS or whatever. Or if you go on a bus, who knows what the other passengers have, and sometimes they're coughing all over the place.

I said I was sure and asked him if he paid cash. He got all offended. He said he was running a real hotel, not a brothel, and I'd get a payslip with all the benefits, and he needs my social insurance number. I told him I don't have one, and he checked on his computer and told me I have to go to an office on de Maisonneuve with my birth certificate, and they'll give me one.

I start the day after tomorrow. Tomorrow I need to get the social insurance number.

He told me his name, but I forget it.

The city is one big skating rink. I poured two bags of salt on the walkway this morning. All I need is for Mrs. Coleville to slip and say it's my fault.

Yours forever,
Fern

Monday
February 11

Hi Xanoth,

I went down to the building on de Maisonneuve, but right at the desk they told me my guardian has to apply for me if I'm under 18.

Now I don't know what to do. What if the guy won't give me the job without a number?

I'm also really stressed about the garbage situation. People are still not following the rules. I'm running out of the black tape, so I called David and asked him for regular tape. An hour later his secretary came over and brought me a whole box filled with pencils, pens, tape, a stapler, a big pad of sticky notes, markers, a stack of paper and a box of white envelopes.

The secretary looked like a model. I wonder if David's going out with her. He never mentions a wife or kids. And there was the way she said, "David told me you needed this." I mean the way she said *David*, I had a feeling she's more than his secretary.

That box of office stuff should have cheered me up, but it didn't. I was too worried about the social insurance number. I made more signs, this time with exclamation marks, and I taped them all over the building again. Louise did the French ones.

I also taped a large sheet of paper and a dangling pencil on my door, and I wrote IF I AM NOT HOME LEAVE YOUR MESSAGE HERE AND I WILL ATTEND TO IT AS SOON AS I CAN.

If I get this job I'm going to be away most of the day and every evening except on Mondays. I really have to find a solution for Beauty.

Yours forever,
Fern

Tuesday
February 12

Hi Xanoth,

I can still work at the hotel. The owner, Karl, said he'll apply for the number for me and he'll say he's my guardian. All I have to do is bring him my birth certificate.

I start tomorrow. With this job, every minute of my day will be filled. Morning: clean building, deal with Mrs. C. Afternoon: hotel. Evening: restaurant. Mondays: put sign on door that says GONE TO OTTAWA FOR THE DAY and pass out.

The good thing is that I think I'll be able to save around $450 a week. That's $1800 a month!

I asked Victor about catsitting. He said, "Sure, babe." I could tell he liked that I asked him.

I said, "It's really important not to let her out," and he said, "I dig it."

So I went out and got a basin at the one-dollar store and filled it with newspaper and cat litter and took it up to Victor with a bag of scraps.

I told Victor I'd clean the litter. All he has to do is

keep Beauty at his place and not let her out. Even when he's away, it's better for her there. It's bigger, and there's a windowsill in the kitchen with a view of trees and grass and people going by.

Beauty was happy right away. Cats can tell if they'll get along with someone. She began inspecting and sniffing and purring, as if she was saying, "Wow, finally I get to go somewhere." Then she jumped on the cozy red blanket and began cleaning herself. Victor stroked her and made faces at her.

I really like Victor. If only I was a normal size and my hair wasn't all stupid and stringy and I had Mom's good features instead of her flat eyebrows and tiny eyelashes, which were fine on her but make me look like Chucky.

I don't mind that Victor forgot about the meal he promised me. Looking after Beauty and being so cool about it is worth a thousand meals. If he's sleeping or at the club when I get home from work, I'll use my janitor's key to get in. Victor doesn't mind. He said, "I got no secrets from you, babe."

Yours forever,
Fern

Wednesday
February 13

Hi Xanoth,

I started at the hotel today. I brought eggplant dip and
pitas and fruit in my knapsack. Karl took me to the
kitchen so I could put the dip in the fridge. I looked at
all the goodies and wondered what Karl does with the
leftovers. He can't always sell exactly every muffin or
piece of cake. I guess he takes the extra stuff home.

It was mostly a training day. Karl showed me how to
do a room. Strip the bed, put on new sheets, collect
garbage and towels, spray, wipe, clean toilet, put in new
shampoo and soap and a glass, vacuum. If the shampoo
or soap is half-used, I can take it home.

I did a trial room while Karl watched. He was
impressed by how fast I was. He talks a lot, but not in an
annoying way. Mostly he talked about his boyfriend
François, who's a lot younger than Karl and likes to stay
out late on weekends. Karl gets jealous but he doesn't like
going out late. But then he wakes up at two in the morning and François isn't there, and he goes to the club to
look for him. And then he sees him dancing and he goes

home and can't fall asleep, so he ends up just as tired as if he'd gone out in the first place.

I was only half listening because I had to concentrate on not making mistakes. Karl doesn't mind. He's like a TV or radio show. It's there if you want to watch or listen to it, but if your mind wanders it's also OK.

There are two receptionists – one for the day and one at night. I won't be meeting the night person, because he comes at eight. The day one is the guy with the purple punk hairdo. His name is Étienne. I like him.

The only other worker at Le Baudelaire is Sally, who does accounts and laundry. She's the sort of person who could be 28 or 38, it's hard to tell. She's medium height, medium weight, medium looks, medium everything except for her personality, which is totally scary. Étienne pretended to tremble when she came into the lobby, and when she left he said, "All clear." He's really funny. He could be an actor. Maybe he really is an actor when he's not being a receptionist. Maybe that's why his hair doesn't fit the rest of him. Maybe he's in a play about punks.

It's going to be really hard dealing with the garbage now that I have three jobs. I don't want to have to wake up before 7:00 in the morning on Tuesdays and Fridays, so when I get home from the restaurant at 12:30 or 1:00 I have to drag a hundred bags to the front.

So my question is, why can't the tenants PUT OUT THEIR GARBAGE IN FRONT TWICE A WEEK? The whole system doesn't make sense. But I can't change it without asking David, and I don't want him to know I'm having trouble with anything.

Also, some people are STILL putting their garbage in small white plastic bags. I'm probably going to have to open one of them and look for envelopes so I can figure out who it is. I can give them some green bags for free if that's a problem. I have lots.

Yours forever,
Fern

Thursday
February 14

Happy Valentine's Day, Xanoth.

Yours forever,
Fern

Saturday
February 16

Hi Xanoth,

Sally told me to take whatever I want from the kitchen!!!

I said, "Karl told me I'm not allowed," and she said, "Yeah, well he's not the accountant, I am." Sally seems to have as much power as Karl, even though she's definitely an employee like me.

Her mood is the problem. The smallest thing sets her off. Like the table for folding laundry is wobbly. Or the coffee's cold. Or there are only two cashews in the mixed nuts bag.

Since she said it was OK, today I helped myself to a small container of chocolate milk, a slice of cake, a poppy-seed cookie and some muffins. I was right. Karl takes home whatever doesn't sell. So if I have an extra muffin all it means is that he's taking home one less muffin. If he catches me, I'll say Sally told me it was OK. But he won't catch me, because you can hear if anyone's coming down the stairs to the kitchen. And Sally does the inventory.

The food comes from a restaurant. It's not the junk

you get in a machine or at the dépanneur. The muffins are really good, with big chunks of cranberries and pineapple. I won't have to bake cakes anymore, if I can have muffins every day.

I'm also stocking up on soap and shampoo and conditioner. I can take anything that's been opened.

Then there's tips. I didn't know that some guests leave tips for the housekeeper. Karl tries to pocket all the tips before I get to the rooms, but sometimes he's busy when a guest leaves and I get to keep the money. There isn't any system. It's survival of the fastest.

I always wear the same thing, jeans and one of my VV shirts, but Étienne describes what I'm wearing as if it's a fashion show. He always finds something to say, like "thrilling russet hues" and "regal collar" and "who can resist that dreamy crepuscular lavender." Crepuscular means twilight.

Tea costs a nickel and coffee costs a quarter, in theory. No one really pays for it. Karl's a coffee addict. I don't know how people can drink coffee. It's just weird bitterness. The booze and chocolates and bags of nuts are behind the front desk and Étienne looks after them. Yesterday he threw me a bag of roasted almonds when I came in and put his finger on his lips. They were divine. I never had roasted almonds before.

I don't feel bad that we're all sneaking things behind Karl's back, especially since he steals my tips. On a full night Karl makes $1,680. Of course he has to pay us and for all the supplies, but it's still pretty good. Besides, I always work an extra half hour at least, so that makes up for the snacks.

Karl's really into keeping the place clean. Being clean is part of being a real hotel and "not a brothel." The worst insult for him is if someone calls his hotel a brothel.

Sally said I can bring my laundry to do at the hotel. I've been washing my things in the bathtub, but it's a problem finding space to hang them. Or finding spare energy. This way I can use the dryer. I'll bring a bit at a time so I don't have to carry a huge bag to the restaurant and so Karl doesn't notice.

I need to open an account at the bank, now that I'm going to be getting payslips. It isn't safe anyhow to leave a lot of cash in this apartment. It could get stolen or destroyed in a fire.

I wonder what a bank account is going to cost.

Yours forever,
Fern

Tuesday
February 19

Hi Xanoth,

Guess who I ran into today – Ricardo! On the metro. He said, "Fern, girl, is that you? What's been happenin?"

I said, "I moved to a new place."

He said, "You still at Sunnyview?" and I said, "No, I work now."

He said, "I'm at LCC, it's murder. You would not believe the homework." Then he said, "That's my stop," but he didn't get off.

I said, "Did you say that was your stop?" and he said, "Yeah, but I gotta get your address first."

So he dug out a pen and wrote my address on the back of a notebook. I said, "How's that girl from Wendy's?" and he didn't even know what I was talking about.

Right then it hit me, Xanoth. It hit me that I don't have those feelings for him anymore. When he left me for the girl from Wendy's I cried and cried, and I was sick with sadness all summer. And now here he was and I didn't feel anything. He was just some guy I once knew.

He said, "I'll drop by one of these days," and I said

right away, "I'm only in Monday evenings and that's when I do my shopping."

I don't want him to come. We have nothing in common, and he'd probably be hoping for the stuff we used to do. The point being?

I guess I'm kind of mad at him too. If it wasn't for him, maybe I wouldn't have been so mean to Mom.

Yours forever,
Fern

Sunday
February 24

Hi Xanoth,

My life has become insane.

The restaurant job is a lot more tiring now, especially if it's a busy night. My boss is really Amir, not Mr. and Mrs. Taza, because if he complains about me I'll get fired. And lately I've been so tired I've been making a lot of mistakes. Yesterday I broke a plate and I set the microwave wrong and I forgot to boil water for tea.

The problem is that I'm making some of the food now. Before I was only heating food up and washing dishes, but now I sometimes have to make the falafel and shawarma and organize food on a plate.

I barely have time to shower, what with all the metro rides and then doing the building in the morning and the stupid garbage twice a week.

I'm still worried about Mrs. Coleville. The other tenants leave messages on the door now and then, like the German student asking if I have oil for the hinges.

But with her it's ten times a day, complaining in her fake British accent about some tomato juice that spilled all over the stairs or the floor creaking or cold air coming in through the windows or her faucet leaking or her sliding closet door falling off. Some things I can't do anything about, like the floor creaking. I can't exactly install wall-to-wall carpets in her place. But I'm supposed to know how to fix a leaking tap or a closet door.

So I called Jeff. He wasn't too friendly, I guess because I didn't give him what he wanted last time. I told him that this time we'll have a chance to get to know each other better.

I don't have a choice. I can't lose this place. I'm really scared Mrs. Coleville is going to call David and tell him I'm never here. When she leaves a message it isn't just once. She keeps calling and repeating the same message over and over. She's furious that she has to wait until the next day to talk to me in person. I've tried calling her from work, but it only makes things worse. She starts interrogating me about why I'm not in the building. At least the noise problem from the apartment next to her seems to have been solved.

I've lost quite a lot of weight. I'm wearing my lowest jeans and they're a bit loose on me, even with one of Mom's belts. It's from all the running around. I'm also eating less because I'm not in charge of my food now. For breakfast I have leftovers from the restaurant and fruit or carrots from the Somerled store. On Mondays I sleep all day and in the evening I go to Somerled for more fruit and vegetables or to Provigo to get litter.

One of these days I'll go to Value Village to look for new jeans. I'd go to a vestiaire, but they don't have a big enough choice, and I'd end up with something dorky from dorkland. I'll try to go on the 50% off day, but the only day I really have time is on Monday. Unless I get to the hotel for 12:30 and leave at 3:30. Then I can take the metro to Namur (4:20), buy the jeans (5:20) and then go to the restaurant. That could work.

Yours forever,
Fern

Monday
February 25

Hi Xanoth,

I got my first payslip on Friday. It was a lot less than I expected. There's all sorts of deductions, like unemployment insurance and taxes. I forgot about taxes.

Anyhow, today I finally went to the bank with the payslip and the rest of my money.

Karl said the bank doesn't charge if you're putting money in. They only charge you for taking it out. He told me to go to Scotiabank because they don't have as many charges and they don't try to screw you.

It's way more complicated than I thought. I had to see a bank advisor to open an account. The bank advisor was a young guy with a crew cut. I told him I'd only be putting money in, not taking it out. He said there were a lot of options, but the one I liked best was where you put in the same amount at regular intervals. If it's locked in, which means I can't take it out, then it's higher interest. The interest is pretty low these days though, so that was disappointing.

He said if I lock my money until I'm 65 I get a tax

deduction, but I told him I'll need the money in around fifteen years.

So in the end I decided I'd put in $650 every two weeks, because you're not allowed to put less than what you decide on. I need some breathing space, in case the hotel closes suddenly, or the restaurant. I'll keep back-up money in my hiding place.

I called Value Village and asked when they were having another 50% off day, but they said not for awhile, because they just had one last week. Darn!

Yours forever,
Fern

Tuesday
February 26

Hi Xanoth,

Jeff came over this morning to fix Mrs. Coleville's tap and door. He found something called a washer in the toolbox and he showed me how to put it in. There's different washers for different types of faucets.

Then he put the door back on the sliding thing, but he said it wasn't too steady because the little wheel is loose.

Mrs. Coleville looked at Jeff like he has bubonic plague. She probably scrubbed wherever he touched as soon as we were gone.

Before Jeff left, he came to my room and we sat on the bed. Luckily he was satisfied with the minimum, which I must say I didn't mind. Also he stroked my hair, which was nice. He's OK. Not my type, but he's an OK guy.

I was late for work because of all this, but if anyone would understand that I got held up by sex it's Karl.

Yours forever,
Fern

Thursday
February 28

Hi Xanoth,

You won't believe what happened. I was doing the
garbage as usual, dragging the bags to the front with the
wind blowing on my face, when suddenly this ambulance
pulls up in front of the building, along with three police
cars. They were there for the mousy woman. Someone
beat her up so bad she almost died. She just managed to
call 911 before passing out.

Probably the criminal walked right by me, and I didn't
notice because I was hauling bags and cursing. He could
have beat me up too, or even killed me.

Friday
February 29

Hi Xanoth,

I only slept four hours last night. The police woke me at seven in the morning. They were asking everyone if they saw or heard anything.

I wanted to beg them not to knock on Mrs. Coleville's door, but of course I couldn't.

Markus answered. He said his mother had taken sleeping pills that "knocked her out," and he didn't hear anything because he was at his computer with headphones.

The police were suspicious when he said "knocked her out." They asked him to wake his mother, but he said she was "dead to the world." That made them even more suspicious, so they asked him whether he would mind coming down to the station to give his statement.

He followed them like a kid who's being taken to eat cotton candy and ride on the ferris wheel at La Ronde. I guess even a police station is La Ronde next to Mrs. Coleville.

Yours forever,
Fern

Monday
March 3

Hi Xanoth,

What a horrible day!

I knew I should tell David what happened right away, but I didn't. I don't know why. I didn't tell him until today. He got so mad! He was really scary. I didn't know he had such a scary side. I guess that's the part he uses in court.

Then, on top of that, he called back an hour later and said he checked the accounts, and the mousy woman is two months late on the rent. He asked me how come I didn't notice that her rent was in arrears. I apologized and promised it wouldn't happen again.

He told me to clear out her stuff and put everything in the cellar. He said he'd come over on Wednesday "to talk." I'm really nervous about that "talk." I don't think he'll fire me, but I'm still scared.

He wanted to come in the afternoon, but I said I had a dentist appointment and I'd be frozen all evening so he said he'd come in the morning. That was fast thinking.

It was really depressing in that woman's apartment.

Just a few pieces of junk furniture, like a chipped TV table with gold legs and a folding chair and hooker dresses in the closet and make-up that looked like the type kids play with, all sticky and gross. There wasn't even a bed, only a bunch of blankets on the floor.

I began to feel really sick, the way I did when Mom died. It was almost like the mousy woman was Mom's ghost.

I'm sorry I was so mean to you, Mom. I'm sorry I'm sorry I'm sorry I'm sorry I'm sorry I'm sorry I'm sorry.

Yours forever,
Fern

Tuesday
March 4

Hi Xanoth,

Victor's ex-wife's been visiting him.

    I finally bought new jeans today. I found a good pair at VV for only $11.99. I made a new rule. Aside from litter, a bus pass, and fresh fruits and vegetables, I'm allowed to spend $15 a month.

Yours forever,
Fern

Wednesday
March 5

Hi Xanoth,

A lucky thing happened. I found David's missing papers in this old battered suitcase on a kind of shelf in the cellar. He was really glad I found them. He opened the suitcase and said in a snide voice, "Unique filing system, heh?" If I ever had any doubts, he definitely does not like his father.

Then he gave me a lecture about telling him things that go on. For my own sake too, he said. To protect myself. But he wasn't mad anymore.

I'm really tired, Xanoth. I feel I could sleep for a whole week straight.

I have to go shovel now. It's snowing again for a change. It's supposed to go on snowing all day.

I don't know what to do about clearing the snow while I'm away. We're supposed to be getting another 20 cm today. This is the snowiest winter ever.

Yours forever,
Fern

Thursday
March 6

Hi Xanoth,

I didn't go to the hotel or the restaurant today. The city's in total chaos because of all the snow. I called Karl and he told me not to bother coming. Then the Tazas called and said the same thing.

Yesterday, the Asian father in the apartment next to me came out while I was clearing the snow and took the shovel from me. He didn't even ask. He just took over without saying a word. I think he was looking out his window and it frustrated him to see me struggling.

So I got this idea to ask him if he could clear the walk while I'm away. I don't know if I'm allowed to ask, but I was desperate. He's always around, because he works at home. Something to do with computers.

He said no problem. He probably needs a break from being cooped up in that small apartment all day.

Yours forever,
Fern

Saturday
March 8

Hi Xanoth,

We had another blizzard today, but I went to Le Baudelaire anyhow, because I didn't want to miss another day's pay. I had to walk backwards from the metro to the hotel.

By the time I finished at the hotel, they were telling everyone not to go out if they didn't need to. I called the Tazas and they said they can't get down to the restaurant from where they live. So I went home. At least I didn't have to take any buses. Traffic was down to a crawl.

The walk from the Snowdon metro was the worst. The wind practically lifted me off the ground, and I couldn't see a thing. It was nice to get home early though.

The Asian father is looking after the walk. I hope David doesn't catch him at it. I really don't know if it's allowed.

I had a long shower and now I'm in bed, with Beauty purring like an engine next to me. It's only seven, but I'm going to sleep.

Yours forever,
Fern

Sunday
March 9

Hi Xanoth,

We've now had the most snow in one winter since 1971.

I saw on the French TV channel how in some places you can actually walk with snowshoes to the roofs of houses. Houses in the country are collapsing from the weight of the snow. And in some parks you can touch the top of the lampposts.

It's hard to shovel because there's nowhere to put the snow. I'll have to wait until they clear the street a bit.

I went to the hotel, but the restaurant is closed again. The snow's costing me more than $200, but at least I'm getting some sleep. And I can still make my $650 at the bank.

Some jobs you don't lose money when there's snow or you're sick. The worse your job, the easier it is to lose it.

Yours forever,
Fern

Wednesday
March 12

Hi Xanoth,

Karl was a wreck today. His boyfriend François walked out on him. He's saying he's going to sell the hotel and either go away or kill himself. He says the hotel will be demolished and turned into condo units, or else it'll become a brothel and crackhouse.

He followed me all day today, talking nonstop about François. He says it was all because of a fight over baked potatoes, because he was too lazy to go out and buy tin foil. He was saying potatoes are just as good without tin foil, and François was saying you need tin foil to keep in the moisture.

Étienne and I tried to tell him that no one dumps you after 12 years just because of potatoes, but he said we don't know François, and if he'd only gone out and bought the tin foil, François wouldn't have left.

I was worried at first, but Étienne said it's not the first time they've had a breakup, and each time it happens Karl says he's going to close the hotel, but he won't do it because he's making too much money on it.

Anyhow, there's going to be a morale-boosting party for Karl on Saturday. I'm invited. I told Étienne I work until midnight, but he said the party only gets going at midnight, and that I can come in late on Sunday. The party's on Côte St. Luc Road, on the other side of Decarie, not far from my old school.

This week there were quite a few small repairs in the building, but the Asian father is helping me out. There was a problem with the light in the hallway, and he got on a ladder and fixed it. He's an engineer, so he knows about things like light.

The other repairs I did myself. A hinge had to be tightened, a kitchen sink had to be cleared with Drano, a toilet got blocked but luckily didn't overflow. I don't think I'll need Jeff again.

Yours forever,
Fern

Thursday
March 13

Hi Xanoth,

David's father finally died.

David isn't sad. If anything he looks relieved. He said, "As soon as the estate is settled I'll be able to hire you properly." That means I passed the trial period.

On the other hand, what if he decides to sell the building and the new owners decide they don't need a janitor?

The couple under Victor left illegally. The ones who thought they were cool. They snuck out during the night without giving notice. They left a huge mess and a lot of stuff. Maybe I'll find something useful.

A divorced woman who's a friend of someone in the building took the apartment right away, so I don't have to show it. I only have to empty it.

The divorced woman came this morning to fill in an application. I forget her name. She looks suicidal, if you ask me.

Yours forever,
Fern

Friday
March 14

Hi Xanoth,

I got good loot from the couple who left – three really nice pictures, a glass salad bowl, wine glasses, a big woven basket, food storage containers, a standing lamp, three wooden chairs, two plants and two drawerfuls of junk that I think they forgot to empty, including two stamps, nail scissors, hair elastics, a loonie, three quarters and two nickels. They also left quite a bit of food.

One of the pictures is a blue clown by Picasso. I really like it. I hung it over my bed. It reminds me a bit of you, Xanoth.

The party on Saturday is BYOB. I don't drink, so I think it's OK if I bring lemonade. It'll have to come out of the $15 I'm allowed to spend this month. I might also be able to sell some of the stuff the couple left.

I may not even go. Everyone there will be cool apart from me. I don't want to be in that situation again.

Yours forever,
Fern

Sunday
March 16

Hi Xanoth,

It's four in the morning but I'm not tired. I just got back from the party to cheer up Karl. Karl didn't need cheering up in the end, because he made up with François, but he had the party anyhow. Sally stayed at the hotel to keep an eye on things. Étienne said she's not the partying type.

I guess I should explain a few things. The first day I went to kindergarten, this girl Arloe Whittaker came up to me and sniffed me and said, "Ugh, you smell like my dog." All the kids began to laugh and they all came over to me and sniffed and held their noses and made that sound UGHH. And that was it for the rest of the year. The kids said I smelled like a toilet, a mud puddle, old garbage – anything they could think of. The teacher, Mrs. Brunet, tried to stop it but she couldn't.

They put all kinds of horrible things in my lunch Mrs. Brunet finally had to put my lunch out of reach to keep it safe. So then they put things in my boots or my coat pocket, like squished food and toilet paper and clay and rocks.

You won't believe this, Xanoth, but Arloe tried to kill me. I swear she's going to end up like Karla Homolka. That's a woman who was a serial killer here on Earth. Arloe even looked a bit like Karla Homolka, come to think of it.

It was right at the end of kindergarten and we were all in the park, and Arloe suddenly pretended to be nice to me. I was so dumb I actually believed that maybe things had changed. She said, "Do you want to play Jesus?" and I nodded and she told me to lie down in this red wagon, and then she pushed the wagon really hard into the street where cars were coming. A car swerved and just missed hitting me.

She didn't even get into trouble. I think Mrs. Brunet was scared of her parents. A kid like that, her parents are probably ogres too.

Then in first grade, this one boy, another future criminal, used to come up to me and whisper, "I'm going to rape you, bagface." He was only six, but he knew exactly what he was talking about.

That was the year Simone left. I sometimes think she left because she knew I was turning into a problem.

By grade two everyone got bored with me because I made myself deaf and I wasn't scared anymore. I went in the opposite direction of my mother.

So even though Étienne is always nice to me and Karl's just Karl, I wasn't sure if I should go to the party. I didn't think people would be mean to me or anything, but I didn't feel like sitting in some corner and being invisible.

Finally I decided to go, but I almost changed my mind again at the elevator. The apartment was in one of these historic type buildings, with carved wreaths under the windows and a courtyard with a mermaid fountain in the middle.

I went into the building and pressed the button for the elevator. As I was waiting, three other people came in laughing and talking. They were dressed in sort of punk, and I was sure they were there for the party.

That's when I almost turned around and went home, but then what would I tell Étienne, so I got on the elevator with them.

As soon as I walked in, Étienne took me around and said, "This is Fern, isn't she fabulous?" Finally he got to this one girl who sort of frowned and said, "We've already met, remember?"

I figured she was someone from Sunnyview, and I thought, this is where it starts. But she said, "I was really worried about you after you left that note. I tried to find you, but no one knew where you moved to. Is your mother OK?"

So then I realized it was Linden, the girl from the rich house. For some reason I didn't recognize her – maybe because she was wearing a raggedy sweater and she looked like she just woke up, with shadows under her eyes and tangled hair.

I said, "She died, actually."

Linden looked shocked. She said, "Oh, I'm so sorry to hear that," and she gave me her phone number on half a napkin and wrote down my number on the other half.

I went over to the table. There was a huge amount of food. I took some bean salad and curry and rice on a plate and I sat down on a chair. People around me were having conversations about movies I never heard of, so I tuned out. But suddenly I realized they were all talking about me.

It turns out that Étienne used to work in a hair salon, and he still does his friends' hair. So they all decided he had to give me a haircut right there and then. I didn't even have a chance to say yes or no. Étienne grabbed a chair and pushed it in front of the kitchen sink and he shampooed my hair while people watched and talked and moved around. It reminded me of when I was a little kid and Simone shampooed my hair in the bath.

When he was finished he wrapped my hair in a towel and there was a long discussion about which style would suit me, with everyone giving different opinions.

I was quite freaked out. I thought maybe it was a trick like "Let's play Jesus" and they were going to give me some horrible haircut on purpose.

This one girl thought short hair would go with my eyes and would look cute on me. That's probably the first time anyone used the word "cute" and my name in the same sentence.

Linden disagreed and said I should have a shaggy cut that reached my shoulders. Étienne kept changing his mind. Finally he brought a magazine and asked me what I wanted. I pretty much went with the shaggy look Linden suggested.

It wasn't a trick. He gave me a really good cut and someone said, "Isn't she adorable?" And even if they were only saying it, it was because they liked me.

Then Linden came over and told me she was going to Sunnyview, which I could hardly believe. We talked about how all the teachers at Sunnyview are just trying to survive with the help of Prozac, except for Mr. Tomorrow, who's on coke. I never talked about a teacher with anyone before. Linden said everyone hates him because he's mean and doesn't teach the right things on purpose so he can fail everyone and feel superior, and I said he doesn't even bother hiding that he's an addict, with his fingernail and runny nose, and how come he doesn't get fired, and she said he can't get fired because of the union. I said I wished I had a union for my jobs.

Maybe if I'd had someone to talk to about school, I would have tried to get something out of it.

Yours forever,
Fern

Tuesday
March 18

Hi Xanoth,

Police again!

Mrs. Coleville had a fit and called them, and I wasn't around to deal with it. I checked my messages from the hotel, and as usual there was this rant from Mrs. Coleville, with an even faker than usual accent. She was going on about how the police came, where was I, what kind of place is this, yak yak yak.

So I phoned her back and I finally figured out that a woman walked in on Victor and his ex-wife, and the two women had a big fight on the stairs and Mrs. Coleville called the police.

What made her really mad was that when they saw the police, they stopped fighting and said it was only a sisterly argument. Mrs. Coleville said they "tricked the police" in order not to get arrested. She was probably hoping for a public execution.

Then she said she wants Victor to be evicted because "those people are nothing but trouble, next thing you know I'll be attacked in my sleep like that woman in

308." She's really playing with half a deck. Étienne could hear every word through the receiver. He made these big eyes and pretended to stab himself and stagger all over the lobby of the hotel.

I finally calmed her down by promising to "inform the landlord and see what can be done." I'm hoping this will stop her from calling David herself.

Yours forever,
Fern

Wednesday
March 19

Hi Xanoth,

The worst news. Just what I was most worried about.
Mrs. Coleville told David that I'm never around. It turns
out she's been spying on me, and keeping track of when
I go out and when I come back. She told him I leave
every day at noon and don't come back until one in the
morning.

So David called, and I had to tell him I have two other
jobs. He said in his tough voice, "I see that I didn't
explain the job to you clearly. You need to be in the
building at least six waking hours a day. This isn't a hotel,
it's a job."

I was beyond stressed. I said, "I'm sorry. I didn't know.
I'll quit one of the jobs. I just have to give a week's notice,
is that OK?"

There was a pause, and finally he said, "All right. By
the way, what's the story with the police coming again?"

He said it like it was my fault. I said, "Mrs. Coleville
gets nervous easily."

He said, "Well, it's your responsibility to keep order in

the building, Fern. If you're not up to it, I'll have to let you go."

I felt like someone punched me in the stomach when he said that. I said, "I'll make sure she doesn't call the police again." But how can I control that lunatic?

I don't know what to do, Xanoth. I'm totally freaking out. David is one complaint away from firing me, and Mrs. Coleville's for sure going to find something to complain about. It's her hobby.

If I lose this place, I'll have to spend half of what I earn on rent, and I'll end up exactly like Mom, in a dead-end job and a dead-end life.

I can't quit the restaurant. It's where I get almost all my food, plus $300 a week. And I can't quit the hotel. I need the money, and it's the first time I've had any friends. I have a week to figure out what to do. Maybe a miracle will happen.

Yours forever,
Fern

Thursday
March 20

Hi Xanoth,

I was just getting ready for bed when I heard something going on in the hall, so I went out to see what it was. Mrs. Coleville was on the stairs in this quilted robe having a huge fight with Victor. I couldn't believe the things she was saying to him. What a racist! I don't even think it's legal to say things like that.

From what I could tell, Victor lent Markus some CDs, and Mrs. Coleville thought it was a trick to get into their apartment and rob them. Victor tried to laugh it off, but when she started with her racism, he got mad, and told her she was an ugly old bitch.

So then she wanted to call the police again. I freaked out. I said, "You can't call the police just because you don't like someone. And if you do, I'll tell them you're the one causing the disturbance."

That really infuriated her, and she started calling me a whore who spends the entire day at a brothel (good thing Karl couldn't hear her). She said she looked up the number I was calling from, and she found out "what kind of establishment" I worked at.

That was when Adorée showed up, wondering what was going on. Mrs. Coleville began spluttering, "And her, her! This entire building is swarming with floozies." Floozies! I never even heard that word, but I got the general drift. "Every day she entertains a male visitor!"

Adorée was really mad. She said, "Shut your face or I'll kick you down the stairs."

I was beyond stressed. I was supposed to keep everyone quiet, and instead it just kept getting worse.

Finally Markus simply handed Victor back the CDs. Victor went upstairs, and Adorée and Mrs. Coleville fumed at each other.

I said, "Why don't we all go back to bed?"

Mrs. Coleville turned on her most bullying voice and said to me, "I'll tell the landlord what you did tonight." Whatever that was.

I said, "We're really doing our best for you, Mrs. Coleville," but she could smell the fear on me and it made her meaner. She said, "We'll see what the landlord has to say tomorrow. It's time we had a decent superintendent in this building."

I completely broke down when she said that, which of course was exactly what she wanted. I ran back to my apartment and turned on the shower so no one would hear me crying.

She wants to destroy my life, Xanoth. What am I going to do?

Yours forever,
Fern

Friday
March 21

Hi Xanoth,

I was late for work today, and so tired I could barely lift the sheets off the beds.

Then at the restaurant I kept dropping things, and twice I started crying. I told them I had a cold, in case they noticed my red eyes. And I left exactly at midnight, even though there were still some dishes. Probably they'll fire me too.

I thought I could do it, Xanoth. I thought I could be a janitor and have two other jobs and that it would all work out, and I wouldn't end up with Mom's life.

But I was wrong.

Yours forever,
Fern

Saturday
March 22

Hi Xanoth,

I was a wreck today. I slept in and didn't do the building at all. What's the point? I'm going to lose this job anyhow.

No sign of Mrs. Coleville. Who knows what she's up to.

Yours forever,
Fern

Sunday
March 23

Hi Xanoth,

David just called. He said, "I hear there's been more trouble, Fern. I can't keep dealing with this."

I told him there was nothing I could do about Mrs. Coleville because she was determined to make trouble. I told him she didn't want any black people in the building.

David sighed. He said, "I'm not saying she's entirely reliable. But I don't have grounds to ask her to leave, which means you have to find a way to keep her quiet."

So I told him how she wanted to call the police again and I stopped her.

David was quiet for a few seconds. Then he said, "All right, I'll have a talk with her."

I hate that my whole life is hanging by a thread. The thread of Mrs. Coleville, the thread of David, the thread of the hotel and restaurant not closing, the thread of Victor looking after Beauty, the thread of not going crazy.

Yours forever,
Fern

Monday
March 24

Hi Xanoth,

Jack's here! Mom's brother!

He showed up at noon yesterday, just as I was leaving for work. He was all emotional, hugging me and so on. He said I look like Mom, and he was all teary. He has hair to his shoulders. On some guys long hair looks derelict but it looks OK on Jack.

I was a bit detached at first. I mean, I don't know him, and when someone's gushing, it's like they're doing the work for both of you. And like if you get into it you're being pulled into their reality instead of staying in yours.

So I was nice but I didn't feel too much. I told him I had to go to work, and right away he started saying he'll find somewhere to stay. I said he could stay here.

So he unrolled a sleeping bag and said he'll sleep on the floor next to the kitchen table. I told him he could have the bed. He reminded me of Mom, how she never wanted to be in the way, and how she used to apologize for the air she was breathing, practically.

He said, "I've learned to accept the gifts that are

offered to me." It's like he has to explain what he does with philosophy.

"You can eat whatever's in the fridge," I said. I don't know if he brought a lot of money with him. I told him there was pita in the freezer that he could heat up in the oven and have with eggplant dip. I forgot to tell him I don't pay for electricity. I can tell he'd worry about that.

He thanked me about a million times and said I had a heart of gold blah blah. He said he hadn't slept in a bed in seven days.

Beauty was hiding under the bureau. I said, "Don't be surprised if a cat suddenly appears. It's Beauty. Whatever you do, don't let her out."

He said, "I look forward to making her acquaintance." Annoying, but he was trying to be friendly.

I was running late, so I left the key on the dresser and Jack took off his shoes and lay down on the bed. He was looking at me with this happy embarrassing smile, like I was some ship that's rescuing him from a desert island he's been trapped on for twenty years. He's going to take some getting used to.

At work I kept remembering that he was in my room, and I hoped he was OK and that no one would see him, especially Mrs. Coleville.

The restaurant wasn't too busy, which meant I didn't have to stay late to finish the pots. Also I got good loot – a ton of rice and falafel. Falafel they only serve fresh, so unless Amir wants what's left over, I get to take it. They already figured out not to throw anything out without asking me first.

I got home from work at one. Jack opened the door as soon as he heard me trying the doorknob. Either he's a very light sleeper, or he was awake. Beauty was on the bed, purring away.

I told Jack I had to do the garbage, and right away he put on his jacket and gloves and came out to help me, which I was ready to love him for right there and then. It was cold and windy as usual, and there's still a ton of snow.

I liked how when we finished dragging the bags, Jack picked up some clean snow with his leather gloves and rubbed his hands together to clean the gloves. A lot of guys don't think about things like that.

I was too tired to talk, so I gave Jack the extra pillow and Mom's quilt to put under his sleeping bag and I had a quick shower and crashed. I told Jack he could shower and it wouldn't wake me. I could tell he hadn't showered or touched anything.

He said no, no, he'd shower in the morning and I should go to sleep and not worry about him. Before I shut the light he said, "The most important thing in life is to search your heart and find the right path." He's reading a book about the right path. Whatever.

Right now it's 9:40 and he's gone out to get coffee at the dépanneur. He's one of those people who has to have coffee in the morning. He had a shower first, though it was exactly three seconds long. I have to tell him the hot water's free. He probably won't take a long shower anyhow, so as not to hog the bathroom.

Yours forever,
Fern

Tuesday
March 25

Hi Xanoth,

Jack bought danishes and bagels for breakfast. We ate together at the table.

He told me about the prison he was at, Rockwood. He was in minimum security, which at Rockwood means you live in cabins that you share with five other people. Jack says Rockwood was a turning point for him. Apart from getting on the right path, he learned computers and first aid and started taking care of his health.

He said that for many years he carried guilt because of the couple on the farm who used to lock Mom in a closet. He was the older one, but there wasn't anything he could do, and it made him bitter, so he drank and did stupid things. But now he knows that guilt and anger eat away at you, and you have to do good to overcome them.

Jack looks a lot like Mom. He moves the way she did and he has a lot of the same expressions. He's really sad he didn't get to see her before she died.

Tuesday (or Wednesday, actually) 3 a.m.

I'm really creeped out, Xanoth. I'm a pretty deep sleeper, but I guess your mind wakes you up if something weird is going on.

It's Jack. He talks in his sleep. He said in this really loud, clear voice, "I'm fixing the hard drive," and "How many megabytes would you say that is?" and "It could be a virus."

It's beyond scary. It's like is it him or isn't it? I almost woke him up and made him go find a hostel or a shelter or something. I mean what do I really know about him? What if he's a serial killer?

I can't even be sure he's really Jack. In murder mysteries you get that all the time. You think someone is one person but they're really someone else. Maybe this guy in my room killed Jack and now he's pretending to be Jack in order to worm his way into my life. Like Jack was hitchhiking and this guy learned all about where he was going and then he killed him and took his money and now he's come to get mine.

I just checked inside the laundry bin in the bathroom. I made sure to shut the door first. The back-up money is still there.

Tomorrow I'm going to ask Jack for proof. I'm going to think of a question only the real Jack would know.

Yours forever,
Fern

Wednesday
March 26

Hi Xanoth,

Jack isn't an impostor. It's easy to go a bit insane in the middle of the night.

Anyhow, we had a long, long talk. We basically talked half the night.

When I came home from the restaurant I was sort of crying because of all the stress I've been having. I was trying not to, but tears kept leaking out of me.

Jack felt terrible when he saw I was crying. Of course he thought it was because of him, and that he should find another place to stay. He thought maybe he was reminding me too much of Mom, or maybe I didn't like having my space invaded.

I said, "No, no, it isn't you. I'm just in this huge mess."

He was all worried when he heard I was in a mess. He probably thought I was involved in drugs or something. I think he was relieved when I explained the whole story of Mrs. Coleville and David and how I have to quit one of my jobs.

Jack was impressed by all the jobs. He said, "You're a

jewel. I always knew it and your mom always knew it."

That got me crying again. He said, "I guess you miss her a lot."

I couldn't take no one knowing the truth, so I told him how mean I was to her. As if it wasn't bad enough that she was stuck with a fat ugly kid everyone hated, I began being a total bitch to her, just like everyone else.

Jack said, "Felicity was proud of you. She told me you were funny and smart and that you looked after everything."

I was suspicious of that. I asked when she told him.

He said she called him on his birthday, and he called her on hers, even when he was in Rockwood. He said she called when I was in school, because she was shy about talking when another person was listening.

Well, that's true. Mom even hated talking to me when anyone else could hear her, which is why she hardly said a word when we went to the IGA or Value Village. The worst thing for her was if the cashier asked her something, and there were other people standing in line. I answered for her half the time.

I told Jack that the last thing I said to her was "Leave me alone, you stupid cow." That's what I said, Xanoth. I said "Leave me alone, you stupid cow." Even though she was only reminding me to take my bus pass.

So Jack took my hand in this really sappy way and said, "Fern, we have to forgive ourselves. We all make mistakes and we all get angry."

I said, "Mom never got angry."

He said, "Well, some people turn anger into sadness. It's explained here in this book I'm reading. Do you want some cheese danishes?"

I was exhausted, but I didn't want to go to sleep so I said OK. Jack took out the danishes and put them on a plate, and while we were eating he said, "Felicity knew you were in a bad mood because of your personal hardship. She said you took over the cleaning when she was sick and you looked after her when she had her migraines. She wouldn't want you to feel bad now. Her spirit wants you to be restful."

I didn't want to hurt his feelings, so I didn't say what I thought, which is that he can't know how she felt when she was alive, and there's no such thing as life after death.

Then he said, "Now about your job problem. Let's see if we can find a way out. Maybe I can take one of your jobs."

"You mean like doing the janitor work?"

Jack shook his head. He said David hired me, not him, and he might not like him. But he said he could try taking one of the other jobs, if they'd agree to hire him. He said we could "pool our resources."

He was right about David. David might even do a search and find out that Jack was in prison. That would for sure be the end of the job for both of us.

Well, Jack can't replace me at the restaurant, because that's where I get my main meal of the day. Also, it's because they know me that they give me extra food to take home.

But he could probably replace me at the hotel during

the week. I don't think Karl would mind, as long as Jack does a good job. And I could still do weekends.

Of course I have no idea if I can count on Jack. He might start drinking again, or he might vanish, or he might not be good at making beds. Or he could die of a heart attack, like Mom.

I asked him what about his plans, but he said, "My plan was to find a job and a place to stay. And here they've both landed at my feet. The right spirit shows you the right path."

I said, "If you don't mind living in one room."

He said, "This apartment has everything I could possibly need. A roof over my head, a shower, a kitchen, and your beautiful company."

I can't remember everything we talked about. He said I gave Mom someone to love and look after, which is the most important thing in life. We were up until almost five.

Basically this might be a solution, unless David decides that Jack can't stay here. If it works, Beauty won't have to be alone when Victor's at the club.

On the other hand, what about the bank deposits? I can't ask Jack to give me his salary. Maybe he'll agree to deposit what he makes into the account, and he can have his part back when I take it all out. Jack's the type to agree to anything.

Yours forever,
Fern

Thursday
March 27

Hi Xanoth,

I found out some things about my father today. Ted.

First, he didn't know Mom was pregnant when he left the farm. He left because the evil people fired him. And the reason they fired him was that he was nice to Mom and tried to defend her.

He liked to travel, and his plan was to go right around the globe. Jack said he was very athletic and he read a lot of science fiction and he liked to draw. He'd sit in a corner after supper with a sketch pad, and draw the imaginary things he read about.

Jack said if he'd known Mom was pregnant, for sure he would have come back, but no one had an address for him.

I'm glad about one thing. He didn't run away from Mom. He didn't leave her because of me.

Yours forever,
Fern

Friday
March 28

Hi Xanoth,

Today Jack came with me to the hotel so I could introduce him to Karl and ask if he could replace me.

On the way to the hotel, I suddenly got into a huge panic again. We were on the metro and I started thinking, who is this person sitting next to me? He was supposed to be my uncle, and he was going to move in with me, but he was a total stranger. A stranger who keeps talking about the right path. I sort of felt sick. It wasn't as bad as when I heard Mom was in the hospital, but it was the same type of feeling.

Then, as soon as we walked up to the hotel, a crossdresser who knows me came out and blew me a kiss and said, "Fern! How are you, sweetheart?"

I could tell Jack was shocked. I forgot to tell him it's a gay hotel, and I realized that the whole concept was going to weird him out. Because I'm from Montreal, but Jack's from a small town. And you forget when you're used to something that it's not the same for everyone. Now it was Jack who was scared about walking into a new reality.

I said, "I forgot to mention that it's the gay village here, so most of the guests are gay. But it's not a brothel." I never thought I'd hear myself repeating Karl's line. "It's a real hotel and I get a payslip with deductions and everything."

Jack said, "People have to find their own path," but he sounded nervous.

Luckily Étienne was his usual hyper self. He said, "My, my, my, my, who have we here?"

Jack shook Étienne's hand and said, "Pleased to meet you." His voice was a bit trembly and I realized that he was anxious about being interviewed and meeting new people.

Karl was already upstairs hunting for tips. Étienne went up to get him and I asked Jack if he wanted coffee, but he said he was fine.

Karl came down and I introduced Jack and asked if we could talk for a minute. Karl said sure and we went into his office. He made himself a cup of coffee and Jack changed his mind and had one too. Poor Jack, his hand was shaking when he lifted the mug.

Karl sank down in his chair on the other side of the messy desk and said, "Just don't tell me you're quitting. It hasn't been a good day so far."

I said, "We were just wondering if my uncle Jack could replace me Tuesdays to Fridays for a while. He'll be great."

Karl didn't even interview Jack. He only asked if the payslips should be made out to me or to Jack!

I showed Jack how to do a room. Then I took him down to the laundry to meet Sally. She was furious of course. She doesn't like anything changing. When we were back upstairs I told Jack not to take it personally. I forgot who I was talking to. "She has her own path to find," Jack said.

At 4:30 I left for the restaurant and Jack stayed on to help Sally fold sheets. When I got home from the restaurant he told me he went out for coffee with her! Wild. He asked her and she agreed. I hope she wasn't too mean to him. Probably no one's asked Sally out in a hundred years and she controlled herself out of shock.

So it looks like it might work out, Xanoth, at least for now. The salary slips are still going to be made out to me, by the way. It saves Sally work, and Jack says the money is in exchange for rent.

Yours forever,
Fern

Friday
April 4

Hi Xanoth,

Things are going OK.

Jack likes working at the hotel and Karl seems happy.
On the home front, Jack replaced Mrs. Coleville's bathroom mirror and the cracked linoleum, so with a bit of
luck she won't complain about him to David, and David
won't complain about the expense or about Jack living in
the apartment. Jack says this is Canada and I'm allowed
to have whoever I want in my apartment, even if I'm a
janitor.

The leftovers from the restaurant should cover most of
Jack's food, and he also brought $200 with him. He
doesn't really eat much. And Karl told him he's planning
to paint the whole hotel, and he's going to hire Jack to do
it.

Every time Jack takes something from me he says, "I'll
accept the good that's offered to me." So he's Mr. Mush,
who cares.

I have more time now, so I took a bus down to my old
library and took out a big stack of mysteries. I don't like

all mysteries. I don't like if they're random. The detective's in love, she isn't in love. The corpse is mutilated, it isn't mutilated. Totally random. Also I need the characters to be smarter than me. Or if they're not smart, they have to be interesting at least. Mostly I take out books that are set in London or Edinburgh or one of those places. I've had better luck with those.

It turns out Jack's the one who gave Mom her moon necklace. I told him she never took it off. He started going on about the moon and its power but I tuned out a bit for that part. I'm not that interested in the power of the moon.

Yours forever,
Fern

Sunday
April 6

Hi Xanoth,

Linden left a message for me on the phone. Something like, "Hi Fern, it's Linden, we were wondering if you could come over for dinner, it's just me and my sisters, my parents are out of town so call me." And she gave me her cell.

I didn't want to go, but Jack said I should. My side: it's pointless, I'm jealous, she's only asking me out of pity, we have nothing in common, the whole thing is random, I don't want to meet her sisters, especially Debbie who left me all those instructions on how to clean the house. I didn't tell Jack all that. I just said it was pointless.

His side: when people reach out to us we have to respond, and there are opportunities and we have to take them, and Linden wouldn't call if she didn't want me to come.

So finally I said I'll go if he comes with me. Why shouldn't he get to eat a great meal in a big house? And if anything goes wrong, at least I won't be on my own.

He said I had to ask Linden because she didn't invite

him, and maybe she didn't want an old guy tagging along, especially when it's all girls getting together.

I called Linden and left a message saying the only time I could come was Monday night and my uncle was staying with me so I thought I'd bring him too and I'll wait to hear from her.

She called me back about an hour later. She said of course it's OK if I bring Jack, and any time Monday was good.

I'm suddenly remembering that Linden's mother gave Mom a copy of *Fifty Ways to Make More Money*. Is that insane or what.

I can't remember what happened to that book. I may have donated it to the trash can.

Yours forever,
Fern

Monday
April 7

Hi Xanoth,

Dinner at Linden's was strange.

We got there at exactly 5:00. I told Jack that Linden was rich, but he didn't realize how rich until he saw the house. He probably only ever saw the inside of a house like that on TV.

Linden opened the door looking as raggedy as ever. She said, "Hi guys, come in, yeah, you know the drill, shoes off or my mother will know through telepathy all the way from Italy. Cool hair." She meant Jack.

We took off our coats and followed her to the kitchen. She said, "Alice is upstairs locked in her room. Debbie's rehearsing with her band but she should be home soon. Sorry about that manic note she left you, Fern. She's obsessive. She can't help it."

She meant the note about how to clean the house. I was surprised that Linden remembered that note and knew how annoying it was.

She told Jack she was sorry about Felicity and how they all liked her. Jack said, "She mentioned your generosity," but Linden didn't seem to hear him. She was really hyper. She poured us this mango-strawberry juice and she brought a bottle of vodka to the table and asked if we wanted her to add it to the juice. Jack got all excited and said, "No, no, I'm finished with that forever." She sat down finally and filled her glass with juice and vodka.

Then her sister came down, Alice. She's 13. She has really curly black hair and she's kind of intense. Linden introduced her and said Alice was into animal rights. Then she said, "Non-human animals, that is. Sorry." I couldn't tell if she was making fun of Alice.

They started talking about whether to wait for Debbie. Linden said the band she's in was rehearsing for a talent show. The band's called A Singer Must Die. I like that name, for a band. Debbie does vocals and plays viola, which is like a big violin. I remember that from a mystery I once read, *Murder After Bach*.

Linden started listing a million things she could either defrost or take out of the fridge – salads, all kinds of pasta, Indian food, different kinds of pizza, and I forget what else.

Jack said anything was fine with him. I said pretty much the same thing. Since it was still early, Linden said we should wait for Debbie, so we followed her to the TV room and sat down on the sofas there.

Linden asked Jack a hundred questions, and he told her things that I was also hearing for the first time. He talked about how he got arrested for stealing a car while he was drunk. He also talked about the farm and what sadists the owners were, not just to him and Mom, but to their own kids too. Once the woman chased her four-year-old around the yard with a carving knife and the kid got so terrified she had a seizure. He said it was a bad place, but it was important not to carry anger blah blah.

Linden and Alice were really interested. Alice didn't say much but you could tell she was listening. Also she did something funny. She like leaned her whole body against Linden. Linden didn't seem to notice and neither did Alice.

All of a sudden Alice got up and went to her room without saying a thing. Linden said, "It used to make me really mad when she did that. But I'm used to it now."

Then she said, "Hold on," and she got up and came back with a huge dark brown coat. She said a designer her mother was getting interviewed with gave her the coat, but it didn't fit any of them. She meant it was too big. She said, "Here, try it on."

Xanoth, it was the most gorgeous coat I've ever seen. It's not real fur, but it looks like a sort of smooth dark pelt and it has this incredible hood and huge pockets and all these zippers inside for putting things so you don't need a purse.

I said it was way too nice for just going around, but Linden said nothing was too nice and that I should take it.

I wasn't sure. I don't exactly know why. But Jack said,

"Thank you, that's very kind of you," before I even accepted it so that was it, I have a new coat. It's really warm and I won't freeze to death now waiting for the bus.

Finally we ran out of things to say and we just sat there in silence. Suddenly Linden said, out of the blue, "I'm so messed up." You can do that when you're rich – say whatever's on your mind.

Jack of course jumped in right away saying, "Things aren't as complicated as we make them. We have to let go of the thoughts that are holding us back."

Just then Debbie came home and they went to the kitchen to start supper.

Debbie's the healthiest person I've ever seen. She has red cheeks and she's tall and athletic. Her viola case was covered with cool stickers.

Linden and Debbie heated up lasagna and tortellini and put five different salads on the table. Finally we all sat down. And then came a strange conversation.

It began with Linden complaining about a note Debbie left her in the morning. Linden said to me, "She doesn't only leave crazy notes for you." She got up and went to the garbage pail under the sink and pulled out a crumpled piece of paper. The note said, IF YOU HEAT OIL, DON'T FORGET TO PUT A TINY BIT OF LETTUCE OR BREAD IN THE PAN SO IT DOESN'T BURST INTO FLAME. LOVE, DEBBIE.

Debbie smiled in a guilty way and said, "Six children –"
Linden interrupted her and said, "Yes, yes. Six chil-

dren died in Montreal in 1990 when two of them over-heated oil."

Debbie said to me and Jack, "If you put in a crust of bread or a tiny piece of a carrot or something, you'll know when the oil starts to sizzle."

Linden said, "Debbie knows the statistics of every type of accident that exists and how many people died of it."

Alice didn't say anything. She was sulking about the shrimp salad.

Jack said, "It's a good trick. More people should know about it."

Then I asked Linden who does the cleaning for them and for the Dixlers now. She said her mother hired a woman from the Philippines, but the Dixlers use a service where it's different people all the time. We began to joke about how sorry we were for those cleaning people, and we explained to Jack about the Dixlers. Alice got angrier and angrier because of the way the Dixlers treat animals. I told them about the gross bugs I saw in the laundry, and Debbie said they're silverfish, which is a perfect name for them.

Alice said that silverfish have been around for 300 million years and they have more rights to the planet than we do.

Linden said the Dixlers are on their fourth dog. The other three all died. Linden said they probably got bitten by one of the tarantulas.

Debbie joked, "Or ate the food," but Alice didn't think it was funny. She got all red and fuming. She said, "Why doesn't someone just kill them?"

Jack said, "There's no point getting angry at one person, because the whole planet's filled with people who are lost."

Alice said, "We've turned Earth into one big concentration camp for non-human life," and Debbie said, "Here goes."

So Alice burst into tears, stormed out, ran upstairs to her room and slammed the door. Jack got up and went after her.

While he was upstairs I said, "I hate that Mom had to work there."

Linden said, "If the world was made up of people like Felicity there wouldn't be war or starvation or pollution."

I said it was only because she was scared of everyone, but Linden said, "No, she was a nice person. Lots of people are scared and it makes them nasty, not nice."

Alice and Jack came back and Jack said something about how great it was that they were all so close, and Linden said her mother read this book that said it's good, if you have three kids, to space them two years and then three years apart, which is why Debbie's 18, Linden's 16 and Alice is 13.

And then she read this book about how it's better for kids to sleep together in one bed, which is why Debbie has a king-size bed.

It got quiet for a few seconds then. I knew Jack was thinking the same thing as me, how different it was for us. And it made us sad to the bottom of our souls.

To get our minds off our thoughts I told them about the woman in my building who keeps on having kid after kid, even though there's no one to support them. I said the kids all sleep together, but they just look grumpy and neglected.

Linden said, "Yeah, it's easier if you have money," but she said it like someone who doesn't have money, not like someone who does.

Then Debbie said, "Daddy says we can get rid of all our money in one afternoon if we give it to the needy people we know, and that either you do that or you don't. And if you don't, that means you're keeping it for yourself and your family, and that's all there is to it."

Linden said Alice would give everything they have to animal charities if she could.

Debbie said, mostly to us, "Mummy says sort of the same thing as Daddy, that it's not her job to fix everything on the planet, and if she got lucky she's not going to complain just because not everyone else is as lucky. She gave all that money to an orphanage in Russia, but that was a PR gig to get her on TV. Her big goal in life is to make sure her brother never gets a penny."

Debbie said that they have to hold on to their money, because there's going to be a global recession. She said there would be a fight for water and people were going to kill each other for it. The strong will kill the weak. And the only people who'll survive will be people who can afford to build themselves fortresses. She said some people already have secret fortresses.

Linden said there was probably going to be a nuclear war and we'd all die horribly. She said there are enough weapons in the world to wipe out the human race a million times over.

Alice said, "You're only trying to justify having money. We're already living inside a glass bubble in the middle of a broken world. We don't have to wait for the apocalypse. The worst thing that ever happened to this planet was humans came. Unfortunately we'll take all other life with us when we go."

I was kind of surprised by how depressing they were all being, considering their lives.

Jack said, "No one knows the future."

We had blueberry pie for dessert and then I said I was tired. I felt suddenly that I had to get out of there. Debbie said she'd drive us home.

Before we left, they forced us to take a silver machine that you can play DVDs on, and Linden gave me some DVDs to watch.

Jack says the machine is worth at least $1000. I said I'd sell it and he said it's wrong to sell a gift. I said it wasn't really a gift. They just had extras and they wanted to even it out. I said the only thing that's wrong is if you're friends with someone only for their gifts.

The coat is a real gift though. I love this coat.

That was my evening. After Debbie let us off, Jack and I did the garbage. It's been really warm the past few days, and the snow's almost all gone. It's exciting to see grass on the lawns, all scrawny but still there, safe and sound. You have to live in Montreal, Xanoth, to understand the feeling of seeing grass for the first time after winter.

The whole dinner already seems like a dream.

I thought Linden and her sisters had a perfect life, but they don't. They're all messed up about being rich and about the future.

I guess no one has a perfect life. But the opposite of perfect – that happens all the time. It's the easiest thing in the world to lose everything. Your home, your job, everything.

I don't want Linden's house anymore, Xanoth. I just want a nice condo apartment with a sunken bathtub. And in winter I'll go somewhere warm, and Jack can come with me.

Yours forever,
Fern

Tuesday
April 22

Hi Xanoth,

I didn't tell you, but I've been visiting Victor pretty regularly, seeing as I have time in the afternoons now. When I come he always says, "Hi babe, what's up and happenin'?" Then he makes us some tea.

I've told him all sorts of things about Mom and my jobs and Jack. I almost told him about you, but I caught myself at the last minute. You're mine alone.

We had a good time today. I talked about my father and Mom and how mean I was to her, and he put on Tracy Chapman's song Baby Can I Hold You. At first I thought she was saying that the only thing a person can do is apologize for what they did, but then I realized she was saying that the only thing a person *can't* do is apologize for what they did. It's impossible to apologize and it's impossible to say you love someone. But it doesn't mean you don't feel it.

That song really made me feel better. The way she says baby can I hold you in that voice of hers. Like she's right there in the room with you, telling you it's OK.

Victor said, "What I like about you, Fern, is you're not complaining all the day long."

Well, I do complain, but I complain to you.

And I complained to Mom.

What Victor doesn't realize is that you have to trust someone and be close to them to complain. You have to trust that they'll still like you. Or that they won't fall apart or begin talking about the right path. Maybe Mom knew that I complained to her because I knew it wouldn't change how she felt about me. She didn't say "I love you," but that's because of her shyness.

Jack's right. Everything she did was to set up a life for me. And if she loved me without saying it, I think she knew I loved her, even though I didn't say it either.

Three people gave notice that they're leaving when their lease ends, so it's going to be busy this week, with all the ads going in.

I probably won't have much time to write, Xanoth. There's a lot going on now in my life, and I need to concentrate on Earth and the people here. They need me and I need them. But even if you don't hear from me as often, I'll be happy knowing you're there, Xanoth, somewhere in the universe, thinking of me.

Yours forever,
Fern

Acknowledgments

Patsy Aldana, the publisher of this book, was immediately taken by Fern's story. I am very grateful for her faith and vision. Shelley Tanaka, my editor, was wonderfully attuned to the way the novel unfolded, and kept me on the right track. Thank you!

Joan Deitch, my fab email friend, read the manuscript and as always had wise and insightful thoughts about it. For many astute suggestions, I am grateful to Derek Fairbridge. My thanks to Shirley Simha Rand for ongoing encouragement. The book benefited from the perceptive comments of her son, Hart.

The Saver is dedicated to my nephew, Joshua. He has a beautiful spirit and great courage. I am proud of him.

My sweet daughter, Larissa, brings me the joy and balance that are essential to creativity, and keeps me in touch with a new world.

Not everyone we meet in our lives is going to be supportive. There will always be people who have too many problems of their own to be understanding and sympathetic. You must choose the right road for yourself, and that means traveling with the right people, too. And if they're not the right people for you, step on the brakes and let them off. Then sail away!

Edeet Ravel (www.edeet.com) has a PhD in Jewish studies from McGill University and an MA in Creative Writing from Concordia. She is the author of a trilogy about the Israeli-Palestinian conflict (*Ten Thousand Lovers*, *A Wall of Light* and *Look for Me*), which has garnered major award recognition, receiving the Hugh MacLennan Prize for Fiction and the Jewish Book Award, as well as nominations for the Governor General's Award, the Giller Prize, the Canada/Caribbean Commonwealth Prize and the Amazon/Books in Canada First Novel Award.

Edeet is also the author of the popular Pauline books for young readers, including *The Thrilling Life of Pauline de Lammermoor*, *The Mysterious Adventures of Pauline Bovary* and *The Secret Journey of Pauline Siddhartha*.

Edeet lives in Guelph, Ontario, with her daughter, Larissa.